Mine

LOVE'S OWN TIMELINE
BOOK TWO

STEPHANIE PHILOMENA

Triggers & Glimmers

'Glimmers and triggers are opposites in that
glimmers spark positive feelings
while triggers spark negative ones.'

Trigger Warnings

MMC was born an addict, and is a former foster child.
His experience was the complete absence of love,
therefore, love coming into his life is new and scary.
Death of a grandmother, cause not mentioned,
off page, nearly twenty-three years prior.
Death of father, cause not mentioned,
off page, nearly two years prior.
Unintentional, minor injury of a puppy,
but I guarantee she's okay and very much loved.

Glimmers

Spring vibes. Think cherry blossoms and kayaking on a lake.
The excitement of a fresh start in life.
The business of opening a bookstore and realizing a dream.
Women supporting women.

Prologue

FEBRUARY 14

The mammoth, yet stunning, bouquet of hot pink roses monopolizes the middle of my coffee table. My best friend November and I have a Valentine's Day tradition of sending each other a bouquet. This year, she sent an extra dozen for no other reason than guilt.

Before Halloween last year, November made a trip to Buffalo, New York to spend some time with her niece. Luck of the draw, she met the love of her life, Rhys, in-flight when they were seated in the same row. She never returned to Los Angeles. Well, she did, but it was only to pack up her apartment. Today, she is unpacking her boxes of books in the custom home library her man gifted to her.

Luck. Of. The. Draw.

Her guilt is uncalled for. I am over the moon that November found true love. Am I thrilled that she now lives across the country in a time zone I have to actually think about before calling? No, because she is my best friend, and was the last person I love to leave California. Yes, because she is outrageously happy and that is all I wish for her.

"Really think about it, Gen, don't brush it aside. You know I'll support you in any way I can. Okay?"

November is high if she thinks I will move to Buffalo, a place I have never even seen except in the photos she texts to me, to open the all-romance bookstore and coffee bar I have dreamt of. I have barely been outside of Los Angeles over the last ten years. I have never touched snow; I wouldn't even know how to deal with that.

"Okay." It's all I can respond, and I know she hears the same noncommittal tone in my voice I hear.

"I love you."

The lump in my best friend's throat is audible, and whether it is a throat lump or eye sting or a sniffle, it is all contagious for me. I need to get off this call before I turn inconsolable.

"I love you too. Talk soon."

The call disconnects as I extend my arm to place my cell phone on the beveled glass of the coffee table. The clink of glass on glass is loud since I rarely put my cell phones in cases. It may sound crazy, but I don't see the point since I have never, ever dropped a phone. Or maybe I like testing fate.

"I definitely wouldn't take this coffee table with me," I joke out loud to myself.

This coffee table is large and I always told myself, if I ever moved to downsize before starting my own business, it would have to go. My sofa? No one could pry it away from me unless they were angling to get hurt in all their soft parts. This sofa was love at first sight when I bought it. Deep navy velvet, high arms and back to snuggle into while reading for hours, and cushy enough to take a nap, if I took naps. November does say it's the best napping place away from her own home.

The glowy, cheerful pink of the roses is a lovely compliment to the velvet. I strain my arm forward to pull one rose free of the wide-mouth vase, capturing a couple drops of water in the palm of my hand. The bloom is picture-perfect.

I settle back into the corner of the sofa, pull my knees up to my chest, and bury my nose into the rose's soft core to breathe in its lemony floral fragrance. As I allow the scent to lift my mood, I look around my large loft apartment. As nice as it has been to live here the last three years, I have lived in mostly smaller spaces in the past. What I think is interesting is, I never got around to buying much for this apartment. Perhaps that's why it has never felt quite like home. Subconsciously, maybe I knew it was temporary.

When I scan the loft, I look through another lens.

What would I take with the sofa?

My great-grandmother's half-circle Singer sewing table that I use as a side table for the sofa. An ornate leaning mirror my mom bought me for a birthday. All the kitchen stuff, because that is expensive to replace. My queen mattress is new, so that is a yes. Wardrobe stuff, after I sift out what I don't wear anymore. And, of course, my precious books. I don't think I could fit all the bookshelves in a new place though.

I couldn't live without my books. Some people will say I'm exaggerating, but they would be highly mistaken. These tomes are full of friends that have seen me through thick and thin and I never tire of their stories. While they are around, I'm not lonely. And moving to a strange place, I will need to lean on them more than ever. November may be there, but I can't rely on her to hold my hand. She travels for business; she has a very full life, especially with her new love.

Wait a minute!

These thoughts can't be swirling around my mind.

Nopity, nope, nope!

I reach for my cell phone and thumbprint it open as I pull it to me.

Preposterous!

I rest my wrists against my legging-clad thighs, hold my cell phone with both hands, and allow my thumbs to roam the screen. Check my emails. Check my Bookstagram.

Don't be ridiculous!

I open Google and painstakingly type . . .

Buffalo, New York.

Asher

His palms itch to open the small moving boxes labeled 'books' piled in several short stacks along the hallway wall; to take a peek inside and satisfy his gnawing curiosity. He wonders what genres these books are. Has he read any of them? Does he want to read any of them? Instead, he locks his front door and heads down the hall in the other direction toward the stairs as to not hold up the elevator for the movers.

'My new neighbor is a reader.'

Chapter One

GENEVIEVE

I can't believe I'm here.

Once I make a decision, I immediately move to planning and implementation. It's not a 'life is too short' thing; it's more 'the only way I will climb this mountain is by taking the first step' thing. I made the move from Los Angeles, California to Buffalo, New York because my best friend, November Day, dangled the proverbial carrot in front of my face that I could open my dream bookstore within my budget in Buffalo. November is the sister of my heart, if not my blood, so living in the same city again was an additional incentive. She herself caught the Buffalo bug, more like the love bug, and moved in with her boyfriend, Rhys Morgan, after a whirlwind romance this past autumn. If you want to get technical, November moved in with Rhys after knowing each other for two weeks, but she didn't leave Los Angeles for good until early February.

November planted the seed for me to move to Buffalo on Valentine's Day. She was a strong manifestor, because after a week of deep dive research, I discovered November was right. I could do it. With the right plan, I could live off my savings to fund and open my bookstore. If I had to apply for a loan, it would be minimal. I could do this on my own.

It was a sunny, yet chilly, Saturday, February 21, when I drank my lavender honey matcha latte while emailing my sixty-day notice to the property management company responsible for my loft. I didn't even bat one of my brown eyes. Next, I opened my web browser to find the best deal on moving boxes, created a list of what I was taking and what I was leaving behind, then booked a moving company without knowing where I was going to live. That apartment search began and ended during a delicious dinner of tortellini, sausage, and kale soup when I texted an address to November for her to take a look-see for me.

I did, however, bat an eye more than once when I drafted my letter of resignation to my employer, saving it in my email drafts until the thirty-day mark. I was leaving behind a six-figure position with amazing benefits on a gamble. My Mexican father and my French mother always instilled in their four children the importance of security and stability, of being able to take care of yourself. Especially when it came to me: the baby of the family and their only daughter. I closed my eyes and could have sworn my spine went cold when I clicked the mouse on send, imagining disappointed expressions on my parents' faces and equally disappointed words coming out of their mouths.

Mea culpa.

"I have too many books for this apartment." My sigh comes right as Stevie Nick's "Leather and Lace" transitions to Simple Minds' "All the Things She Said" in the low volume unpacking soundtrack that has been playing all morning. "Before I left LA, I stuffed all the little free libraries with books I could easily replace if I wanted. The only books I brought were the special ones."

November is the tried and truest of friends. She's leaving for a work trip tomorrow yet has been helping me unpack for the last two days. We saved the books for last and grouped them according to author on the immaculate maple wood flooring in front of the white IKEA Billy bookshelves we assembled yesterday.

"Genevieve! There are over a hundred books here. Who am I kidding? Nearly three, maybe." She holds up two copies of the same book and snorts. "You have duplicates in some of these boxes."

I avert my eyes and continue shelving my prized Ali Hazelwood collection, stacking and angling each book trophy just so. "Then one copy is signed and the other is my reading copy."

"You have special editions of the same book."

"I had the space in my last apartment." *And a lot of disposable income.* "Maybe I can use the spares for event giveaways at my bookstore."

"If I didn't know any better, I would say you only moved to that loft to accommodate your growing library."

It's my turn to snort. "If I did, it was done unconsciously."

November shifts from her knees to a cross-legged position on a corner of the large, soft area rug we rolled out before my navy velvet sofa was brought in by the movers. Her eyes scan the bookshelves, then the book stacks we created, and I know the next words that are about to come out of her rosy lipped mouth. Words I don't want to hear.

"My dear, you don't have enough shelf space. Even if we stack books decoratively around the apartment, you still don't have enough room."

Books are just as important to November as they are to me, and she sounds very sorry to break this news.

I feel my lips form a frown. "I guess I could put some of

my reading copies on the shelves I saw across from the elevator. It looked like a little free library but on a larger scale."

"I know you like to have your books nearby, but I can store some in my home library."

"If I was jealous of anything you have, it's that library of yours. Or a man who gifts custom libraries."

She stifles a giggle. "You make it sound like I'm Belle, and Rhys is the Beast."

"Huh." I shrug. "You're right."

I take a good look around. The living room furniture is perfectly situated with the exception of needing to buy a coffee table. I was right to leave the old one behind, as I originally thought. It would have been massive for this space. But the sewing table with its iron scrollwork legs fits well as a side table to my glorious sofa. My new white kitchen looks clean and organized as if I've been living here for months already. I trusted November to handle unpacking the kitchen while I took care of my bedroom and bathroom. We operate similarly when cooking and baking and I knew she would set me up right. All that needs to be done is organizing the bookshelves and placing their boxes in the recycling bin. Maybe a light vacuuming.

I check the time on my cell phone. "Hey, Em! It's past two o'clock. You should go home and pack."

She looks up as she pulls three remaining books from a box: one by Danica Nava and two by Susan Lee.

"Rhys is packing me as we speak." Her smile is an automatic reaction to speaking his name.

"You have the ideal man, you know." I know she knows.

"Oh, I know. Every single day."

I stand from my own cross-legged position and immediately feel the torture of moving I've put my body through the last few weeks.

"Still. You need to go home. Check on things. Be with your man the remainder of the day. I'll take care of the books tonight."

Her resignation shows in her body even though she beats it back on her face.

"I feel bad leaving you here."

"Why?" I ask as I extend my hand to help her up.

She places her hand in mine. I simultaneously hoist as she pops up. Her long, dark ponytail bounces behind her.

"Because I made you move here and now I'm abandoning you for almost two weeks."

"Em, you didn't make me do anything. You should know better than anyone that no one can make me do anything."

"But I'm going to be gone. You've never really been out of California."

I have to laugh. "Oh dearest! You make it sound like you're leaving me in the middle of a jungle with no sat phone." I shake my cell phone in front of her. "Have GPS, will travel."

She exhales audibly. "You're right, but I still feel bad."

"You have to work. Life goes on. And think about all you and Rhys will see in Montana and the road trip home. I'm glad the two of you are squeezing in a fun vacation. This trip was planned long before my plans to move."

"I have always wanted to see Yellowstone, but it's still going to be cold there. I would rather have gone in June, but this is the date the client chose. You're lucky you missed the snow here. It was a hard adjustment for me. Rhys did say it has been known to snow this deep into spring."

"I'm not ready to learn to drive in snow yet, so hopefully I brought the sunshine with me." I quickly mull it over. "I am excited to see snow though."

November pauses and she looks at her black grip socks that have 'LOVE' printed on top. I know she's about to shift the conversation to something deeper than snow.

She looks up and meets my eyes. "I think I already know the answer, but have you told your family you moved yet?"

"You definitely know that answer."

"Why not?"

Before I can answer she places a reassuring hand on my bicep and continues, "I was at that Thanksgiving dinner when you brought up the idea of opening a bookstore and your brothers were belittling a-holes. Your mom told them to stop, but didn't really say much else because your dad took over. He was much more caring in his advice of hanging onto your job and how you have a good life and wondering if you could compete with Amazon and Barnes & Noble." November is careful treading on Dad because she knows his death still feels fresh even after a year. "Not one member of your family thought it was a good idea. I feel you may be stuck at that dinner table, but, honey, that was a few years ago."

I remember November gripping my hand under the table, lending me her strength, because she knew I wanted to cry. My family loves me, but they all want the baby of the family, the only daughter, in a gilded cage.

"I am stuck there. I didn't know they would react that way. I thought they would push back, but I thought they would be open to hearing me out."

"It was harsh to watch. Their opinions didn't deter you, but I don't understand why you haven't told them you're here."

I blow out a breath and place my hands on my hips. "Because I didn't want this chapter to be ruined for me. I already have thoughts about this move and everything that could go wrong; I don't need an echo of that."

November pulls me into a tight hug. "Honey, you have to yank the Band-Aid off."

"I'll tell them soon."

The background music morphs to another song that happens to be one of my mother's favorites: "I Just Want to Be Your Everything" by Andy Gibb.

We pull apart.

My eyes go wide.

November's eyes go wide.

We grab hands and begin to dance in the disco style my parents used to lovingly groove to when this song would play. And my best friend and I laugh when we make mistakes in our steps, and even when we don't.

Secretly, I love this song too. And I'm happy our time together is ending on an up note.

If it weren't for GPS, I wouldn't have any clue where I am, yet the directions to Trader Joe's are easy enough. I selected driving side streets just to see what I could of the changing neighborhoods along Niagara Falls Boulevard. When November plugged the from and to addresses into my GPS before we parted ways, she said she and Rhys will take me to see the actual Falls when the temperatures turn warmer and all the attractions are open. We'll play tourists, one of the things I loved to do when I lived in LA.

Toto, I've a feeling we're not in Kansas anymore.

I most definitely am not.

One thing that's fantabulous about Buffalo? It doesn't seem to take long to get anywhere. I know I'm not close to my new home, but it feels close when I turn into the parking area and find a space near the Trader Joe's entrance. That will be helpful in case it starts to rain again, which by the speckles on my windshield, it will. I'd rather not get my groceries wet, but I'm loving the rain here–such a rarity in LA.

When I step outside my white hybrid Lexus SUV, the chilled wind whips through my long curls. My bare fingers have to wrestle my hair out of my face. I can't imagine how I look to any onlookers.

I have a lot of hair.

Back into my car I go, partially closing the door for the few moments it takes for me to sweep my hair up with my hands to the top of my head and twist it in a bun of submission. Satisfied I'll be able to see as I walk door to door, I hurry through the biting air to yank a red shopping cart free from its stall, then push it into the welcoming warmth of Trader Joe's.

The only food items I brought with me from Los Angeles are my collection of spices and some Mexican ingredients November said I would need to get through any homesick feelings that might crop up. That said, my cart is heavy and overflowing. I need everything! Baking ingredients. Condiments. Dairy products (mainly cheese). Lots of frozen veggies and other items, including ice cream. Stuff for salads. Stuff for soups. Nuts. Fruit. Cherry vanilla sparkling water. Chocolate. And those damn chili lime tortilla chip thingies. This is the most money I have ever spent in one shopping trip at Trader Joe's since I started living on my own, but I am so grateful the store is here in the Buffalo area. It's that little bit of familiarity when everything else is so new.

I drive the quicker route home via freeway . . . I mean thruway. I'm starting to feel the weight of the move sink into my bones and I'm exhausted. It also doesn't help listening to the hazy music of "Back to Friends" by Sombr on low volume through the car speakers. But after I park in the secured parking under the apartment building, I realize I have too many bags to carry at once to the elevator. I pull out of my space and sidle up as close as possible to the elevator doors, quickly unload my car, then repark. Luckily, this is a smallish building and I'm not far away, but I still trot back.

When the elevator doors open, I press the lock button and move like lightning to shove all the grocery bags inside before the buzzer can sound. I glance over my shoulder to make sure I haven't forgotten anything then press the release button and level two. There's less than a minute for me to sag against the interior metal wall.

Must push through!

The elevator stops, and I bend to grab four bags, two in each hand, to ready for a fast unloading. I'm glad there's no ding sound when the doors open as my apartment is close by. I'm a light sleeper and would definitely be aware of the noise. I press the lock button and step into the small lobby where the little free library shelves are located.

I'm surprised to see a rather tall man sitting on the espresso brown commercial carpet, his long denim-clad legs bent in front of him, black Converse sneakers planted on the floor, back against the ivory painted wall. I can't see his face, but I can see hair that is dark brown without being too dark, not long and not short, wavy and not wavy, maybe messy, maybe not. He's slow to look up from his book that rests against his knees. I recognize the distinctive blue of the paperback cover: *Book Lovers* by Emily Henry.

My extra copy of *Book Lovers* by Emily Henry.

The elevator begins its angry buzz screeching at me that I'm taking too long and snaps me back to my task.

"Merde," I mumble.

Easing all the bags to the floor, since I forgot which one the two dozen of eggs are in, I turn back to grab the remaining bags. In the seconds it takes for me to turn back around, the man is on his feet, stepping over to . . . I don't know, help me?

Man, is he tall.

Once I clear the doors, the man reaches a long arm inside to press the release button, then pulls back before the door slides closed. He turns his body to face me.

"I'm Asher. Do you need help?"

Asher isn't smiling, but his voice is not unfriendly. If I had to guess, from my thirty-five years on this planet and the observant creature I am, his nature is serious. He may be an introvert. If he's reading on the floor of a lobby, definitely a bookworm. And I feel nor see any threat from his body language.

I set the brown paper bags down then extend my right hand to Asher. "I'm Genevieve."

Asher's hand engulfs mine, not because he's beefy, but because I'm five-foot-four and he has to be a whole foot taller than I am. My hands are in proportion to my body and so are his. But his hand is warm. His handshake is both firm and gentle-maybe I'm wrong or maybe I'm right, but I feel Asher is a nice guy.

When I look up at his face, his fair skin suits him and behind the Clark Kent-style eyeglasses, I see the prettiest hazel eyes I have ever seen on a man. Too bad he's most likely a neighbor in the building. I don't date where I live. More so, he's totally not my type. Too young. Too casual. I normally date men who are older than I am, wear suits for work, and don't dare have their hair touching their collars or covering their ears. Well, that was the type of man I had plenty of access to while I worked in a prominent Beverly

Hills law firm. Not that I indulged in any workplace romances, but all the peripheral men were fair game. Regardless, I'm not looking to date anyone right now. Opening my bookstore comes first and that will suck up all my time.

"I think you're my new neighbor," Asher states in his deep, and not quite deep, voice.

Asher: the man of this and not quite that.

'Or maybe you shouldn't make assumptions,' as my dad would say.

Asher continues, "I saw the moving boxes near your front door. We share the same vestibule."

"So, you're the door next to mine."

"Yes." Asher shifts his weight from one foot to the other and holds out the book to me. "Are you the one who added to the shelves?"

"I didn't have enough room for all my books, so . . ." I gesture with my hand toward the shelves then bring my arm back to my side. "Are you enjoying the book so far?"

"When I came home, I noticed all the color on the shelves. My books pale in comparison; lots of black and white spines. I saw the words *Book Lovers* and I'm a book lover, so I took a look. It's different from what I usually read, but I like the author's voice."

My hand gestures to the shelves again. "Is all of this your doing?"

I can't put my finger on it, but I can almost feel Asher retreat into himself.

Is he shy?

"I read a lot and don't want to become a complete hoarder."

I can't stop the chuckle that escapes me. "I know the struggle well."

Asher glances down at my bags. "I'm heading back to

my apartment. I'll help you carry these, if that's okay with you."

His manners are impeccable. "Thanks. After the last few days, I can use the help."

Asher tucks my book, his book, the book under his left arm and stoops down to pick up the two heaviest bags in his left hand and three bags in the other like they weigh nothing. This makes me reassess his build which I originally thought was lanky but now see as athletic with broad shoulders under his plain navy crewneck sweater and original wash jeans.

I retrieve my house keys from my right jacket pocket before picking up the remaining three bags, the lightest on my right arm, as Asher waits for me to walk ahead of him. Thankfully, our vestibule is just around the corner, and after I unlock my door, Asher manages to hold it open for me to pass through. I lead him to the kitchen and set the bags on the floor which he mimics.

"I really appreciate your help, Asher. Nice to know I have a good neighbor."

There's that retreat again.

"Sure. If you need anything, I work from home most days."

"What kind of work do you do?"

Retreat. Retreat. Retreat.

He does not like talking about himself.

His body angles to leave. "Computer stuff mostly."

Somehow, that tracks.

I can feel the discomfort wafting off him, and I unexplainably feel bad I can't make him feel comfortable in my presence. I'm usually good with people, with putting them at ease.

"Well, that goes both ways, Asher. If you need anything, just give my door a knock. And after you read *Book Lovers* and like it, I suggest reading *Beach Read* next. Or try something by Ali Hazelwood."

"It was nice meeting you, Genevieve."

"You too. And thanks again for helping me shlep."

I think I see the tiniest twitch of his lips, but it also could be what I want to see. I'll never know for sure, because Asher is gone.

Asher

Out in the hall, after locking his front door, Asher turns and stares at Genevieve's closed front door as he places his earbuds in his ears. He hasn't seen her in a couple days, yet he has thought a few times about how relatively easy it was to make small talk with her. And for reasons he can't understand, he wonders if it would be just as easy to have longer conversations with her.

He turns away to head outdoors for an early morning run, and switches on one of the many workout playlists he created for himself. "Mayonnaise" by Smashing Pumpkins opens to its grind of electric guitar and heavy bass when Asher continues to wonder.

Or would it be like it is with everyone else?

Chapter Two

Nothing for two days.

More like my body screamed 'ENOUGH!'

Two days ago, after I ate my pint of banana pudding ice cream while organizing my bookshelves (I did need to decoratively stack some books on the sewing table, but no more than that), I showered and crashed. I don't think I made it to nine o'clock that night. When I woke up at seven a.m., it was pouring rain outside and I couldn't tell if there was a part of my body that didn't hurt. That's what happens when you carry too many boxes, move around furniture until it's in the perfect spot, and are constantly bending and squatting and lifting without a break.

After peeing, brushing my teeth, and taking two Advil, I went into the kitchen and made myself a tray of snacks and beverages and went back to my bedroom. Carrying that tray felt like my arms might fall off, but I made it. I pulled the ivory silk blackout drapes back from the one floor-to-ceiling window and climbed back into bed where I stayed for the majority of the day listening though my metallic pink headphones to *Savor It* by Tarah DeWitt for my, probably, twelfth time now.

Did I mention I live by a river? I'm talking, if my building moved forty feet, it would topple into the Buffalo River. It was one of the selling points for me to sign the lease. But the view is complicated. This building is a renovated warehouse or factory or something else from a long, long time ago. Therefore, my view is, yes, of a river, but upon each side are old factories and granaries, some repurposed, some not. It's gritty, yet fascinating. It stirs a need to explore inside me. To learn about where I am. To see what my new home city is all about. I wondered if it was wanderlust I was feeling as I chewed a bite of warm cinnamon toast.

Yesterday, the clouds squeezed out more raindrops but began to move along by noon. I took more Advil and felt better enough to attempt to bend my body into a few yoga poses on the living room rug. The stretch was that tightrope between pleasure and pain—the hurt that feels so good. Muscles still aching, but feeling loose enough, I got to work on what areas of the city I would investigate for potential bookstore locations.

November and Rhys gave me some leads, but I need to see everything for myself. My bookstore, like most businesses, would have certain needs like available parking, visibility from the street, and clientele potential. But also, a feeling. I want to go to work every day and feel like I made the right decision. That this gamble was worth it. For that, I need to do some driving around to explore.

When I pull the drapes back this morning, my eyes form reactive slits; the sun is so bright. I immediately dress myself for a day of exploring. I would have gone out even if it were raining, but it will be much better not looking through the back and forth of windshield wipers and streaks of water. So much better since pretty much every street and sign and building is new to me.

I make myself a quick fried egg sandwich with mashed avocado, savory chicken sausage, and arugula on a seeded bun. Vanilla matcha latte on the side. I sit on one of the backless, camel-colored leather stools at the kitchen counter to eat while mapping the towns furthest away to investigate today. I'm nearly done with my sandwich when what was sunshine illuminating my apartment turns shadowy.

No! The weather app showed no clouds like this!

I don't need to turn fully around to see the monstrosity out of the corner of my eye.

What the actual f-

My eyes go wide when I'm standing and facing the windows.

A ship.

A massive ship is gliding by my window.

Is this real?

I hurry to the glass door to my balcony and quickly slide it open, barely registering the chill on the breeze as I step outside. I scarcely notice the dampness from the rain remnants seeping through my socks that I will need to change before I leave. But I one hundred percent notice this gigantic ship gliding by . . . with very little sound. I hear some water lapping against the rocks below, but you think you would hear more. And I don't see anyone aboard. A ghost ship of sorts, this is.

"It's a lake freighter."

I hear the vaguely familiar male voice to my left and turn toward it.

Asher, in his glasses and wearing a charcoal gray crewneck sweater with a slightly lighter wash pair of jeans this time, is sitting in an outdoor armchair, the only one on his balcony, open book in hand, and a mug of something on the side table.

"A what?"

"A lake freighter. They carry and deliver cargo via the Port of Buffalo."

"I've never seen anything like it. I feel like I can reach out and touch it. Is this river even deep enough?" I think a half a second. "Scratch that. Of course, it is."

Asher casts a glance over his shoulder to the front of the freighter then points that direction before looking to me again. "You can see a tugboat ahead, guiding the freighter through the deeper parts of the river."

The ship is so long, it's still passing by. It's the lower middle section, but it still is higher than my apartment level.

"Do they come through often? The freighters? What do they deliver?"

He shrugs. "Could be anything from sugar to cement. There are still working factories here, like General Mills on the other side of the river. And the freighters don't come through often."

The ship is still passing by. Still virtually soundless. Still a thrill to see.

"This is . . ." I have no words to finish that sentence, but I know seeing this when I do will never get old.

I turn to face Asher, and I can spot a tiny glimpse of the tugboat just to the side of his head. I also spot the book he's reading and it's not the blue of *Book Lovers*.

"You are either a fast reader, or *Book Lovers* didn't do it for you."

Asher looks down at his book then holds it up so I can plainly see the cover. *Bride* by Ali Hazelwood.

"Fast enough. I liked *Book Lovers*. When I returned it to the shelf, my intent was to read *Beach Read* like you suggested, but this caught my eye and I remember you mentioning this author."

"She's one of my favorites for too many reasons to get into now. How are you liking it so far?"

He looks down at the book for a long moment, as if to gather which thoughts to mention. Perhaps he doesn't want to hurt my feelings because the book is not his cup of tea, yet I notice he's nearly halfway through, so . . . does he not DNF books?

Picking up the plain silver bookmark that rested beside his mug, he says, "I understand Misery more than I want to. Not the vampire part, obviously, but a bit of her life."

He secures the bookmark inside *Bride* before snapping it shut. I watch as he picks up his mug as he stands.

I'm not sure what to say to that remark, probably because it's not what I expected to hear and I'm not at all sure what he means. Misery leads a solitary life, one without a whole lot of love. Asher takes steps toward his door but stops before going inside. "I have to start my workday now. Have a good day, Genevieve."

He means it. It's his tone of voice that tells me so, yet his somber expression is immovable.

"You have a good day too, Asher."

I mean it as well.

Rhys had mentioned that the main arterial streets in Buffalo branch out quite a distance into the suburbs. If you drive any one of them from a suburb, you will end up in down-town Buffalo. I drove the thruway out. Now, I'm driving Main Street back home.

No luck.

That's okay. I have only scratched the surface of the

plethora of locations to scout. Like this area I'm passing through right now. Super cute with all the restaurants and boutiques. Everything here looks independently owned. Charming.

Wait a minute!

I spot two signs at once. One for Glen Falls something. The other a for-lease sign on a small, single-story building just a short distance away.

Without thinking of cars behind me, I brake in order to make a sudden right turn down a side street near the Glen Falls sign. Fortunately for me, no one was close behind me.

I love driving here!

I find a space at the curb to park and excitedly jump out of my SUV to see an actual waterfall in the middle of a main street in the middle of a town. And it's no little trickle of a fall. No, this is gushing water. I am giddy!

Holy cow!

The scene is strange to me. The sky is picturesque, robin's egg blue with the occasional puffy white cloud passing by. The sunshine is warm through the cold breeze. I am surrounded by water and spring green and homes down the way and parkland. This couldn't be a more different place than I'm used to in its beauty and oddity.

My eyes spot a glimpse of the building that interested me and I head up the sloped sidewalk back to Main Street, then cross the bridge over the waterfall to the building. At first look, it needs quite a bit of work, starting with a good power-wash. After a closer look, I see the endless possibility of what this building can transform into. The square footage seems to be what I'm looking for. There's ample parking, walking traffic, the residential neighborhood behind, plenty of other businesses on the busy street. The building has huge display windows, which I'm nearly pressed against, trying my best to keep my clothes away from the grime, to get a better look inside. The space has mass potential.

The sound of the waterfall seeps into my ears and I'm drawn to the side of the building. And I see it. Imagine it. I could have outdoor seating; it would overlook the falls, maybe enclose it during the cold months. Add fairy lights along the railings and from above somehow.

Did I just find my location???

I don't wait. I extract my cell phone from my purple tote bag as I step back to the for-lease sign to plug the phone number into the keypad. It rings once, twice, before a woman with a singsong voice answers my call.

"Good morning. Oh my! I mean good afternoon. You have reached Gold Realty. I'm Anne. How may I assist you?"

"Hi. My name is Genevieve and I'm standing in front of a building on Main Street with one of your 'for-lease' signs. I'm not seeing a street number, but it's the building right next to Glen Falls. Are you able to give me more information? I'd be happy to come to your office today to discuss."

"Oh, I am so sorry, but the lease was signed recently, and we haven't had a chance to swing by to take the sign down. I am so sorry to waste your time."

The lump in my throat grows larger as I feel the crash of immense disappointment from the walking on clouds sensation I was only seconds ago experiencing.

"Thank you for letting me know. Have a good day," I manage to speak before disconnecting the call.

This 'have a good day' is one of only politeness.

When I'm blue, I bake.

Once my front door is shut and locked, I place my tote

bag on a hook on the wall. I step in my kitchen and wash my hands with the foamy lemon soap from the dispenser next to the faucet. The fragrant bubbles inspire me to bake lemon streusel muffins to brighten my mood. By the time I slide the muffin tin into the pre-heated oven, my disappointment has diminished.

Of course it wouldn't be that easy.

I set the timer on my cell phone as I step out onto my now-dry balcony. The day definitely got warmer; too warm for the thick sweater I'm wearing. The water below is glinting in the sun. Everything looks the same as this morning except for the absence of the ship and Asher.

I stare at the furniture on his balcony. One chair. He must not have a lot of company over. I assess the dimensions of my own. I really should measure before shopping, but I can already picture two small, but comfy, chairs and a small dining table. It will be nice to have breakfast out here in the summer and another option to dine when November comes to visit. I picture talking to Asher about books over the space between our metal railings.

When my cell phone alerts me it's time to pull the muffins out of the oven, I'm feeling much more cheerful, hopeful even. And as I place the muffins on the cooling rack I set up on the counter, it dawns on me that I have no one to give muffins to. I have a dozen delicious muffins that just don't taste as good when you freeze and thaw them. I usually take extras to work, but I don't have coworkers anymore. November and Rhys are out of town. I don't have anyone.

I know . . .

First, I need to get out of this sweater.

Asher

Asher can hear her through their shared wall, especially when she's in the kitchen like now. The whir of an electric mixer. The shutting of an oven door. Though foreign, it's not unpleasant. He listens to the sounds instead of music, and he suddenly notices he is more aware of one person than he has been in his life.

Chapter Three

GENEVIEVE

Oh, God! Is he going to think I dressed up for him?

Asher saw what I was wearing this morning and now, I've changed into a purple sundress with a daffodil yellow cardigan and white canvas Keds. I haven't knocked yet. I could go back into my apartment and change into something else. But this outfit makes me feel good and I really need to feel good rig-

My knock isn't necessary because Asher's front door is wide open. He nearly collides with me as he is about to step out but halts. Surprise wreaks havoc all over his face. A face without eyeglasses. The first time I'm seeing him without eyeglasses. I momentarily try to decide which look is more handsome, until I squash those thoughts entirely. He fills the doorway with his height and the breadth of his shoulders.

And I think I might be blushing. *Can't be!*

I realize my fist is still in the air, ready to knock, and I lower it to join my other hand holding the small linen-lined breadbasket, then jut the basket out to Asher.

"I baked muffins without thinking about quantity.

You're the only person I know in town. Sort of know." *Awkward!* "They're lemon streusel."

Asher gingerly takes the basket from my hands and looks at the gift. His expression has morphed from surprise to something much softer I can't define.

"Thank you," he says quietly. "They sound and smell delicious."

It's then I notice the camera bag hanging from his right shoulder.

"You're welcome. Is that a real camera you have there? I don't think I know anyone who owns a camera. Except maybe my parents back in the day."

He looks down at his bag as if he forgot it was there.

"Yeah. I'm going to Delaware Park to see the cherry blossoms. The festival was this past weekend, so they should still be plentiful. I thought I would take pictures before they're gone."

Before I can stop them, the words are out of the gate. "Would it be okay if I tag along?"

Asher runs his fingers through his hair.

I backpedal. "I'm sure you want to do this solo. It's okay. Maybe I'll go when I'm out and about tomorrow."

"No!" I think he surprises himself at how loud he is, like he has never heard his voice at this level even though I wouldn't consider it loud. "I mean, it's no trouble for you to come along."

I study him a few moments just to make sure he is being truthful and not polite. When I'm satisfied, I nod.

"Let me grab my tote bag and I'll meet you at the elevator."

"Okay. I'll put away the muffins. Five minutes enough for you?"

"I'll be ready in less than two," I say as I take the three steps to my front door.

Shockingly, it does only take me a little over a minute to gather what I need in my tote bag and stop at the coat closet to grab the picnic blanket off the top shelf. I am so glad I decided not to leave this behind when I moved.

I finish swiping my lips with my Coca-Cola Cherry Lip Smacker, cap it, then hear the tube hit the package of Red Vines in my tote as I round the corner to the elevator. Asher is already there, hands stuffed in his jeans pockets, looking so boyishly awkward, I have to smile.

He smiles in return. It's a small smile, but I'll take it.

Asher drives a big, well-taken-care-of or possibly new, charcoal gray pickup truck that my short self wonders how I am going to climb into it as we approach. I guess this size vehicle makes sense for his height, his long legs, and all the snow in winter. He opens the passenger side door for me, then lends me his hand to help me step up. It radiates Mr. Darcy vibes. I wipe that ridiculousness out of my head as he closes the door when I'm safely inside.

His hand is surprisingly calloused for a man who does 'computer stuff.'

The ride to Delaware Park is quiet, sprinkled with Asher pointing out various streets that lead to various sights, and me asking follow up questions about said sights. Neither of us speak about anything personal and I'm quite okay with that. I don't know why, but I really don't want this new experience tainted by talking about the big city I used to live in. It might come off as a snobby comparison, and I'm not that person.

After parking on a side street at the curb in a residential neighborhood, I am floored with the sheer size of these homes. Some three stories. Some expansive. All looking like they belong in a different time of long ago. All beautiful in their own way.

"Who lives in these houses? Are they single-family homes?" I have to ask.

"Just people. Some are singles, but some have been renovated into apartments. As you get to know the city, you'll see most of the massive mansions have been turned into businesses or medical facilities or schools. On Elmwood, there is an old castle-like property that used to be a psychiatric facility but is now a hotel. There's a small museum inside that exhibits the building history along with some other prominent buildings."

We stop at a crosswalk, looking both ways before we continue across the wide street.

"Interesting. I really need to be a tourist and see everything."

Asher looks down to me. "You are today."

I nod before turning my head forward again. There is a great big white building that looks like something that should be located in Washington DC.

"What is that?"

"It was renamed a few years ago, but I still know it as the Albright-Knox Art Gallery. I think it's Buffalo something Art Museum."

"Whatever it is, it's stunning."

"If architecture is your thing, you'll be impressed with what this city has to offer. And there is plenty of history in the most unexpected places. A few streets north of us is Fordham Drive. Just a normal residential neighborhood for this area and on the grassy median is a small plaque on a rock that marks the place where President McKinley was assassinated during the Pan-American Exposition in 1901."

"That is unexpected." I can't even wrap my brain

around how old this city is. Adding to the never-ending list of things to google.

On the other side of the street, we navigate toward a staircase by another charming building with pillars in front and look like they go all around. I read the small sign over the entrance and, oddly, recognize the name. *Is that the restaurant November had her first date with Rhys?*

Halfway down the cement stairs, Asher stops and turns toward me.

"Genevieve, I'm so sorry. I didn't ask if you were up for a walk. If you aren't, there's a parking lot at the Buffalo History Museum where we're headed."

"Please! You have no idea how much fun this is for me."

To prove my point, I skip down the remaining stairs but stop at the bottom because I don't know which direction we're going. If the smear of cherry blossom pink I see on the other side of this beautiful lake is any indication, we're going left. As soon as Asher catches up to me, that's exactly where he guides me.

We are not the only ones out in this sprawling park today. It's a weekday and I'm sure the vast majority of people living in this city are attending to their daily duties, but there are those that are enjoying the warm sunshine here in this beauty of nature. I'm equally grateful and triggered I don't have a job. I try to remind myself that this break won't last once I find a home for my bookstore.

Hopefully.

I spy what I think is The Buffalo History Museum that Asher was referring to on the other side of the lake. The cherry blossoms against the light gray of the building and the intense spring green of the grass and other trees along the lake's edge look like a watercolor painting. We arrive at our destination, our walk becoming a stroll, and, well, the cherry blossom trees are breathtaking with their dainty blooms. Some catch a ride on the breeze, making the air look like how I imagine snow falling.

"Do you like it?"

Asher's voice stirs me from my revery, yet I can't take my eyes off the trees.

"Like is so insignificant a word, Asher. I have seen nothing like this."

"Do you want to walk around the park some more? See some of the museum? What would you like to do?"

My eyeballs finally look up to Asher, who is studying my face with those intense hazel eyes, patiently awaiting my answer.

Eyeglasses? No eyeglasses? Stop it!

"Asher, I'm the hitchhiker here. You do you. I am perfectly capable of entertaining myself and there is a lot here to entertain me. I'll be close by. Find me when you're done."

He looks hesitant. "Are you sure?"

"One hundred percent. Go take your pictures."

We part ways, but I do stick to the area. I can wander the park another time. The cherry blossoms have a limited life, and I want to absorb their beauty like a sponge.

I find a patch of grass on a mild slope that looks like it has dried from the last rain and spread the blanket I brought and very appreciative of its waterproof backing. I make myself comfortable under the tree canopy, sitting with my bare legs tucked under me for a bit of warmth. Now that I'm sitting still, I feel how cool the breeze is. My dress is long but not a thick cotton. Luckily, my cardigan is keeping my arms protected, and I can fold the blanket over me if I start shivering. The last thing I need is Asher to see me cold and have us leave before he's done. I may not know him very well, but I do know he's that kind of guy who would place my well-being over anything he wants to do.

I pull out my paperback copy of *Done and Dusted* from my tote's large front pocket. I'm only doing rereads now as to not distract me from the work I need to get done. Since I know the story's outcome, I don't have the hyper need to know what's going to happen next. Every now and then, a blossom falls on the page I'm reading that I gently pick up and place on the blanket. The blossoms that land on my hair or an arm or the skirt of my dress I leave, because they make me feel like I'm living in a dream.

The next blossom that rains down, I slip my cowgirl print "Save a Horse (Ride a Cowboy)" bookmark on my current page before closing the book. The blossoms want me to pay attention to them, but my eyes immediately spot Asher.

He's wearing a marine blue Henley shirt that is a striking match against the pink blossoms. Asher is focused, taking his time hunting for and snapping each shot. As he aims, I try to imagine what he's seeing through the lens. Sometimes, he gets up close to a branch with a particular cluster of blossoms that has caught his eye.

I feel like I am understanding him through my own lens. Asher is definitely an introvert. Shy. At certain moments, not wholly comfortable in his skin. Yet, here, he is not shy in his art. I watch him claim each shot without a thought of who might be watching him. He angles. He leans, squats, kneels–owning his space. Cherry blossoms cling to his hair, a few to his shirt, making a home on him because they know he would do them no harm. And I agree.

The air is disturbed by a gust of wind that is crisper than the breezes, and I do shiver. That same wind that passes me reaches Asher, mussing his hair even more, and grabs his attention. Lowering his camera, he looks directly at me as if he has always been aware of where I am. He walks to me, stopping at the edge of my blanket. He crouches down because I know he doesn't want to tower over me.

"Are you ready to go?" he asks as he packs his camera away.

"I'm okay if you need to take more pictures. It's lovely here. I'm not bored if that's what you're thinking."

I raise my book to show him I brought a backup plan. When the laminated bookmark slips out and falls to the blue and cream plaid blanket, Asher picks it up before it can blow away. He glances at the words before handing the bookmark back to me, comically raising one eyebrow as I take it from him. It's the most expression I've seen him make to date.

The heat in my cheeks is embarrassing. "It's a cowboy romance thing."

"First, a bookish romance. Then a vampire werewolf romance. Now, I have to sample a cowboy romance. Anything else?"

I shove my book and mark into my tote bag. "So many, but I'm sure you want to get back to your own books."

He cocks his head to the side. Whether I prefer with eyeglasses or without, one thing is for sure: Asher really does have the most beautiful eyes I have ever seen on a man. A fascinating blue-green like the color of the lake before us with shards of amber and gold bursting out from the pupil.

"Why would you think that?"

"I don't know." Honestly, I really don't. If he wants to continue on this romance journey, I welcome it and will give him all the recommendations until he's sick of me.

Asher stands, then holds out his hand to help me stand.

That barely-a-smile of his appears. "I like expanding my horizons."

My leg and core muscles are strong. I can stand on my own easily, but his chivalry is too good to pass up. It makes me wonder what man or woman in his life taught him the little acts of politeness. His mother? His father?

"And it's paranormal romance," I say as I take his hand and rise to my feet.

"What?" Asher gathers, shakes, and folds the blanket as I dust myself off.

"The vampire werewolf romance is called a paranormal romance."

"There's a subgenre for vampires and werewolves getting together?"

I reach to take the blanket from him, but he continues to hold it as he begins to walk in the direction from where we came. I follow, taking a few quick steps to walk beside him.

"It's not just for vampires and werewolves. Paranormal romance covers other beings, even ghosts."

His eyebrows bunch together as he shakes his head. "Is it ghost and ghost? Ghost and human? What?"

"Oh Asher! You have soooooo much to learn!" I can't hold back the giggles at this adorably charming man.

Asher

Asher uploads from camera to desktop computer the photographs he took on Wednesday. As "In Your Eyes" by Peter Gabriel plays through his desktop speaker, he flips through each photo, deleting the ones he deems not worth a save, until he comes to the first of three he took of her. The first is a wide shot with the lake in the background, boughs of cherry blossoms above, and her back to the camera. She's standing, taking in the view, the skirt of her purple dress rippling in the breeze. The next photo is of her sitting on the plaid blanket she spread out on the grass. She's reading a book while cherry blossoms cling to her curls. The last picture is her book in her lap and her face lifted toward the trees, the sweetest smile adding to her look of wonder.

He saves all three pictures.

Chapter Four

GENEVIEVE

I t's the first day of May. A Friday. The middle of spring. April showers, bringing May flowers and all that. But you know what May first means to me? It's rent day. An in-your-face reminder that I have no income stream yet and I am failing in my quest to get one.

Don't panic! Don't panic! Don't panic!

I'm sitting on my balcony with my laptop open in front of me, logged into the property management resident portal and doing the responsible adult thing in paying my rent. This task is responsible, but I'm not feeling responsible in this moment of thinking about the secure job I left in Los Angeles that provided me stability. Not a worry in the world.

Yet, when my mom's voice, my dad's voice aren't trilling through my head about providing for myself, when I search for that tiny, desperate whisper about following dreams and not having regrets at the end of my life, I close my eyes and make all the noise quiet like November has taught me. I imagine all that self-doubt drain through my body and into the ground below to be alchemized by Mother Earth.

Breathe.

As if I conjured her, my phone vibrates against the butterfly mosaic glass tabletop. A text. It's eight a.m. here, so maybe six a.m. in Montana. November and Rhys are guests at a large resort and spa where my friend is doing her kickass thing teaching corporate people how to work-life balance. And her doting boyfriend is awaiting the time when it's just the two of them. Rhys is so incredibly good to her, and vice versa, that it solidifies for me never to settle for anything less.

How's everything going?

Been exploring. Settling in.

No location yet?

Nope.

The ellipsis bounces a couple times, then stops and a few seconds later, November rings through. I place one earbud into my right ear and accept the call.

"Hi!" I try to sound not so much cheery, just normal.

"What's wrong?"

So much for trying to outsmart my sister. "I know it's early days, but I thought I would have found a location by now."

"Nothing at all?"

"Well, I did find a perfect location right next to that waterfall you told me about on Main Street."

"What happened?"

"It was already leased, and they hadn't taken the sign down yet."

"Nooooooooo."

"Maybe it's the waterfall's fault, because nothing seems to compare."

"Was it that perfect?"

"Did I mention the waterfall?"

"I am so sorry, Gen."

"It's not your fault. Don't worry. The right space will come."

"But this is you, and I know you have to be stressed."

The last thing I want is November to stress now. I know she's chewing her bottom lip. I know she thinks she's at fault for 'making me' move to Buffalo. But I am an adult with agency of my own life and choices. I had to follow this dream.

"No worries! The space that's meant for me will come. So, give that lower lip of yours a rest."

I'm pretty sure I hear the faint pop of her releasing that lip from her teeth.

"Yes, the bookstore will come. I know it will happen for you, Gen. We both just want it so badly when what we need is to be patient."

"Yes, patience."

She sighs audibly. "Still. I can understand why you can't get past the waterfall."

"Right? Seriously, I had this whole seating area planned at the side of the store with that view and fairy lights."

"Oh! Fairy lights! I can totally picture this."

We both let out a sigh.

I look out over the river to the horizon of Lake Erie beyond and I can't help but feel the sensation of optimism charge through me. Filling my reservoir with possibility.

"I can do this." My voice sounds as if I believe it.

"Yes. You absolutely can."

November's voice sounds like it too.

Asher

In the bright morning light, Asher sits at his home office desk, staring at his computer. On Sundays, he likes to get a head start on his work week. The brilliant thing about working for himself is he accomplishes what he needs to on whatever day. Unless he's traveling for work, his days are his own. When he works, he's focused. Yet, today, sitting in front of his desktop computer, fingers idle above the keyboard, he wonders what she's doing on the other side of this wall.

Chapter Five

GENEVIEVE

My Sundays were all routine back in Los Angeles: a longer workout of Peloton and weightlifting in the morning; double condition my hair and the long skincare regimen; meal prep; housecleaning; and reading until bedtime.

Sundays here are a mix of old and new and being adaptable. I still Peloton and go downstairs to the small gym in my building to lift weights. I still double condition my curls. But today's skincare routine was short, because I wanted to go out and investigate another section of the city.

As charming as it is in this pocket on the West Side, the available retail spaces are tiny for what I need. I did find a bakery that offered homemade pop tarts and chocolate hazelnut croissants, so no need to stress bake when I'm home. Instead, I opt for pulling out ingredients to make comfort food: chicken enchiladas in red sauce and a pot of beans.

When I turn off my Vitamix full of homemade sauce, I hear my phone ringing, and the sound of Edith Piaf's voice can only indicate it's my mother calling.

About three months after my father died, my mother made the decision to move to Paris to live with her sister. Los Angeles had too many heartbreaking memories for her and she needed a fresh start, to go back to the country she was born and raised.

"Life moves in cycles," said the woman I get the pink tone of my skin from to my father's tawny. "Going back to France is the completion of this cycle for me."

She took what mementos she wanted with her, then left me and my brothers to sort through everything else for what we wanted with instructions to donate what remained. The house was paid off, so after the sale and paying taxes, Maman split the money evenly among her kids. It's that money plus my own savings that I'm living on now and will pay for the start of my bookstore.

As I fumble to place an earbud in, I quickly calculate the time difference in my head. Since my mom still has no idea I have moved, she thinks it's noon in California, but it's actually 3:00 p.m. here. 8:00 p.m. in Paris.

I press Accept. "Bonsoir, Maman!"

"Bonjour, ma chérie. Comment ça va?"

"Ça va bien. Et toi?"

"Bien, bien. You sound tired. Is something wrong?"

I pour the thin red sauce out of the blender pitcher, scraping down the sides with a thin silicone spatula.

"Just the Sunday Scaries." *I hate lying by omission.*

"God, I hate that term. Sundays are what you make them to be." She tsks. "My daughter works so hard. It's early for you. Why don't you have a siesta?"

For the decades my mother lived in the United States, her accent has never waned. I'm glad for it, because her voice sounds like a melody to me. And hearing her throw in a Spanish word is soothing and heart-wrenching, bringing me back to all my family members at home together. A time when my father was still alive and everyone was living in the same city.

I rinse the pitcher then fill it with warm water and a little dish soap to soak. "You know I'm not great at napping. I'll just go to bed early. Besides, I just made enchilada sauce."

"My mouth is watering. Red or green?"

"Red. And I have a pot of black beans simmering on the stove."

I check the corn tortillas I set out to thaw on a strip of paper towels. November is an angel for telling me to bring Mexican ingredients with me, but these few packages of tortillas aren't going to last forever. I know how to make my own, and I have a tortilla press, but it's not my favorite thing to do.

"Delicious! I know your father loved pintos more, but I'm with you in preferring black beans. That's why I always made both."

"After Dad taught you how to make beans." I lift the heavy lid of the sapphire blue Staub pot with my left hand, and watch the steam waft upward, before stirring the dark beans concoction with a wooden spoon.

"Your father was a great cook. Just not a good baker."

"Mexican dinners with French desserts," I lament as I close the lid.

"It's a better combination than one would think."

The sigh at the end of her sentence makes me think she's talking more about her relationship with my father than food, and I feel the sting behind my eyes burn.

Don't cry! Don't cry! You will not make Mom sad by crying!

She continues, shaking off the bittersweet memories, "Any plans for the week? Are you dating anyone new?"

"Non, non." I begin the task of shredding the roasted chicken breasts that are now cool to the touch.

"Ma chérie, you will not find love sitting on the sofa reading a book."

This makes me smile. "Au contraire! I read romance; therefore, I find amour all the time."

She tsks me again. "You know exactly what I mean."

"I know. I just need a break and to focus on work right now."

"Work isn't everything."

"What about all the speeches about responsibility and taking care of myself I've heard all my life?" I tease.

"I don't like to know you're all alone in that city, especially since November moved away. How is November by the way?"

Guilt gnaws my guts. "November is fantastic! I wouldn't be surprised if she and Rhys are married by this time next year."

"Je suis heureuse pour elle. Tell her hello for me."

"I will. Tell Tatie I love her."

"I will. Je t'aime."

"Je t'aime, Maman."

With a clean pinkie, I disconnect the call.

As I continue to finish shredding the chicken, my vision becomes watery and my stomach doesn't feel as excited to eat the food I'm preparing.

I fucked up. I should have come clean.

Next time.

Asher

There's an imaginary itch to Asher's skin he can't comprehend. A need to pace the floor. A gnawing he can't diagnose. He tries to concentrate on a complex string of code he would like to complete before the end of the day, but he hears music coming from her side of their shared wall. It's faint yet unmistakable. He would know any of those songs from any of the soundtracks just from a few bars hummed. And it beckons to him.

When Asher exits his front door, he smells something familiar. Something good. Something from his time at Stanford. His mouth waters and his stomach rumbles. And it's all because of her.

Chapter Six

GENEVIEVE

After a few weeks of scouting, I think I have a decent enough knowledge of Buffalo and its surrounding towns to narrow my search to a few areas that would suit my bookstore. Instead of going out today, I spend my morning searching the online commercial real estate ads to see if there is any fresh meat on the market. It's Monday and I had hopes, yet nothing for me. The real estate agent Rhys put me in touch with only knows of suitable listings opening this summer. If I have to wait that long, I guess I have no choice. There are houses available that might be zoned for commercial use, but it's so much riskier to spend that kind of money and I would have to take out a loan.

The good news is, it's May fourth. (You would think it was Cinco de Mayo with all the Mexican food I made yesterday.)

May the fourth be with you!

I have been a fan of the *Star Wars* movies for as long as I can remember. My brothers' influence for sure, but even as an adult, I still make time to watch two or three movies on this fan holiday. Who am I kidding? I watch these movies year-round, but this is the day every year I schedule the movies with snacks.

I felt too sick to my stomach to eat the food I made yesterday. Today, my guilt diminished, I made a large portion of guacamole, poured blue corn tortilla chips into a big bowl, pulled the salsa out of the refrigerator, then set it all on a tray on my brand-new coffee table. Actually, it's an old tan leather steamer trunk I bought at an estate sale. I only stopped because I was dying to see inside a real Victorian home and came out lugging this trunk behind me. It was in good condition and after I gave it a thorough cleaning, I was pleased with my purchase. It looks great with my sofa.

The enchiladas won't be ready for about twenty minutes, so I take a seat and begin *Rogue One*. I'm on my second guacamole-laden chip when there's a knock on my front door. I hit pause on the TV remote, chew quickly and take a sip of water before heading to the door. I see Asher through the peephole and don't hesitate to open the door.

"Hey!" I hear how sparkly my voice is and realize I haven't seen him since our trip to Delaware Park last week.

Did I scare him off? I thought we had a nice time. I shouldn't have butt in on his excursion.

"Hey!" His voice isn't sparkly, but he does sound curious. And his eyeglasses have returned. "Are you watching a movie?"

I feel my eyes widen. "Is the volume too high? I'm so sorry to bother you, Asher."

He shakes his head. "No, I was wondering if you're watching a *Star Wars* movie."

"Yeah, I just started *Rogue One*."

"I love that movie."

"I think it might be my favorite. Do you want to come in and watch with me?"

"I-" He jams his hands into his jeans pockets and doesn't seem to know how to answer.

I open the door wider and stand to the side to give him plenty of room to walk through.

"Come in, Asher. It's May fourth, and I need someone to celebrate this great day with. And help me eat the ton of Mexican food I made."

"I really don't want to intrude."

"After I intruded on Wednesday, you are welcome to intrude today. So, come watch *Star Wars* movies and eat some food. Okay?" I drum my fingers against the door expectantly.

Asher steps inside and by the time I have closed the door after him, he has already toed his sneakers off and is standing, waiting for me in his white-socked feet.

The timer on my cell phone chimes, signaling the enchiladas are ready. I turn off the alarm, slip my hands into oven mitts, and proceed to open the oven door.

"Can I help you with anything?" Asher asks.

"You can help yourself to something to drink from the refrigerator. Glasses are in the upper cabinet to the right of the sink." I pull up a corner of the aluminum foil covering the large glass baking dish. The cheese is bubbling goodness. "Will you pull out two dinner plates too?"

As I set the baking dish on top of the stove, I hear dishes clink against the quartz countertop. We work seamlessly around each other as I grab serving utensils; he busies himself in the refrigerator pouring himself a glass of water from the Brita spout. I scoop refried black beans from the hot cast iron pan and add to our plates; he pulls out the small containers of sour cream and chopped green onion I asked for which he sets on the counter and uncovers. I add two enchiladas to each plate; he opens a couple drawers looking for the dinner forks. We both spoon a dollop of sour cream on our enchiladas and sprinkle green onion on top. It's all a smooth dance, even in this small kitchen.

We bring our food to the living area and settle in on the sofa.

Asher looks around. "I like how you decorated your apartment. I didn't really see it when I was last in here. When I'm done with the books you set out in the lobby, I'm going to take a look at these shelves, I mean, if you don't mind."

I think that's the boldest Asher has ever been, and it makes me happy he's starting to feel comfortable around me.

"You can borrow my books anytime, except the special editions. Those are never to be read, but I have reading copies."

Asher extracts a chip from its bowl and scoops up some guacamole. "I know better."

Did he just deadpan tease me?

I don't have a chance to ask.

"Did you make this guacamole yourself?" He doesn't look at me.

"I did. Does that mean you like it?"

"It's the best I've ever had."

I watch him pick up his fork, and there is undeniable anticipation on his face. He takes a bite of an enchilada and his eyes flutter shut. I feel like taking a victory lap around the apartment.

He swallows. "Genevieve, this is incredible."

I'm gooey inside from his praise. I feel like a preening cartoon character.

"My dad taught me to make the sauce. I cheated with the tortillas and chips, but I made everything else myself.

This is food I grew up with. Mexican food from my dad's side of the family, French dishes and desserts from my mom's side."

Asher forks another bite and looks at me like there are a hundred thoughts turning over in his brain. He offers none of them.

"Are you ready to watch the movie?" I ask, because maybe I don't want questions right now. I basically lied to my mother yesterday and don't want to stir up those guilty feelings again.

He nods as he chews a first bite of beans.

I pick up the remote and push play. "There's plenty of food, so if you want more, I'll pause the movie."

"This is the best Mexican food I've ever had. Thank you for inviting me in."

I cast a glance his way, but his eyes are already on the TV screen.

"You're welcome, Asher."

We watch *Star Wars: A New Hope* after *Rogue One*, and we each have two helpings of food by the time the sun has started to set. Asher helps me clear the coffee table and he loads the dishwasher while I place the leftovers into smaller Pyrex dishes I used to use for meal prepping. We talk about the movies and make plans to watch *The Empire Strikes Back* together at some point soon.

"I'll host next time," Asher states as he slips on his sneakers.

I hold out two of the lidded glass containers for him to take home.

"I'm going on a work trip to DC in the morning and will be gone for a few days. I don't want the food to go to waste," he explains for not taking the food.

"Enchiladas freeze well."

There's that look on his face that I can't seem to grasp. I

don't know him well enough to understand his quiet expressions yet. In time, I will.

"Since you're here alone, let me give you my cell phone number just in case you need anything."

That wasn't what I was expecting to come out of his mouth at all.

He takes the dishes from me as I pull my phone from my right legging thigh pocket and hand it to him unlocked. Dishes balanced in his left hand, he easily and quickly types his information into my phone using only his thumb. When he hands it back, I see he even added his last name 'Adams.' I send him a quick text, but I don't hear anything sound that he received it and it must show on my face.

"I wasn't planning on being here long. My phone is in my apartment." He pulls his house keys from his right front pocket before stepping toward and opening the front door.

I take the door from him, watching as he steps into the vestibule and turns to face me.

"Thank you, Genevieve." The corners of his lips turn up in a soft smile. "I had fun hanging out with you."

"I did too." My smile is wider. "Have a safe trip."

His whole face turns soft, and I feel like it's too much for him to show me, so he looks away and steps toward his door. I close mine.

Not even a minute later, my phone pings with a text.

Have a good night, Genevieve.

You too, Asher.

I can't help the giddiness and glee pooling inside me over having a new friend, because that's exactly what Asher is quickly becoming to me.

Asher

Asher lays wide awake in his luxurious hotel bed, unable to shut his brain off. Usually, he doesn't mind work trips. He focuses and completes whatever is required of him. Since his last trip to New York City with his friend, Gareth, he's learned to explore the city he's in during his off hours. Here in DC, he catches the last of the cherry blossoms and views the monuments and memorials in the evening. All of it new and interesting to him. Yet Asher feels an unprecedented desire to return home.

Chapter Seven

GENEVIEVE

The next few days are a blur of sameness. Wake up. Workout. Shower. Breakfast on my balcony while I read or take in the view. Run any errands or jump right into work. First, I check the retail space ads, then research potential local vendors and artisans to stock the gift shop section of my bookstore. Check out bookish shops online and social media for the latest trends. What's working? What's not? I eat lunch, usually leftovers from whatever I made the night before for dinner or a big salad. More work. Reading. Dinner. Reading. Skincare. Bed.

For breakfast on Friday, I eat an egg scramble with red bell pepper, spinach, tomato, and a little shredded mozzarella. Drink coffee with unsweetened vanilla almond milk this morning. No reading this morning. It looks like it might rain today and I'm enjoying sitting on my balcony, watching the gray clouds crowd the sky, allowing only glimpses of sunlight through.

I haven't seen any freighters pass by since that first one, but I also haven't been sticking to the window like glue. I've seen more small boats and kayakers on the water lately. Right now, my eyes watch a kayaker paddle fluidly from the direction of the Lake Erie. It's hypnotic. The rhythm of the paddle strokes at a relaxed pace. As the figure grows larger, I can make out it's a man wearing a life vest on a bright blue kayak. He expertly steers the kayak toward the far end of the apartment building and disappears. The jagged rocks block my view.

When the man appears again, he's vestless, carrying the long kayak on his right shoulder, and walking the wide strip of pavement in the direction of my balcony. It's unquestionable who this man is.

Well, now you know one way he stays fit.

I wave.

Asher waves.

I wait until he's within speaking range, allowing my eyes to wander over the kayak, his long sleeve heather gray T-shirt, and slate gray board shorts. His bare legs are athletic, like someone who exercises regularly. He has a rower's body, a strong one, if not struggling to carry that big kayak is any indication.

Yes, I'm aware I'm ogling. I never said he wasn't attractive.

"I didn't know you were home."

He stops below my balcony. "I arrived late last night."

"Yet here you are, up early and getting in some exercise." I nod to the kayak. "That looks like fun."

"If you want to come out with me, let me know."

"I don't know how."

"I'll teach you."

"Is there somewhere I can rent equipment?"

He looks down at the ground for a moment, thinking, then his eyes are on me again.

"Yes, but I have a kayak you can use."

"You have an extra kayak?"

"I . . . do." He seems unsure for some reason. "How tall are you?"

"Five foot four." He must need to know if his spare will fit.

"That works. It will be raining this weekend, so maybe we can begin lessons next week."

"I'm excited!" My voice, and the movement of my face, my clapping, reflect it.

I get that soft smile in return. *Maybe that's the only smile he has?* I find it odd that I want more. I want teeth. I want to hear what his laugh sounds like.

"Are you free later?" His volume lowers, or maybe it's the wind carrying it away. "Would you like to come over to watch *Empire*?"

If I didn't know better, it almost sounds like he's asking me on a date, but I do know better.

"Sounds good to me."

"Do you like Chinese food?"

"Very much."

He nods. "I know the best restaurant. I'll pick up dinner. Anything in particular you want?"

"I'll eat it all." *Not a lie.* "You decide."

"I have some work to take care from my trip. Is six o'clock good for you?"

My phone vibrates against the table.

"Perfect. See you then."

He shifts the kayak a bit higher on his shoulder and starts his trek again. "See you then."

I pick up my phone to see a text from November.

> Are you free for brunch on Sunday at my house?

> Yes. Are you home now?

My phone rings and I stand, breakfast plate in hand, to take the call inside because it might be hard to hear over some gusts of wind. I press Accept as I step inside, leaving the door open behind me for some fresh air, and head to the kitchen.

"So, are you home?"

"Not yet, miss me?"

"Madly!"

"Miss you more."

"Hi, Gen!" Rhys greets me to let me know I'm on speaker.

"Hi, Rhys! Where are you?"

He replies, "We're driving the northern route. I'm not a hundred percent where we are, but I do know we are in Michigan close to the Canadian border. The weather is decent, so we may drive straight through Ontario, then home. It all depends on how hard it rains, though."

"Aren't you two going to be too exhausted to host a brunch on Sunday?"

November answers, "We're having food brought in. We miss all of you and want to get back on track with family Sunday brunches."

"Okay. What time and can I bring anything?"

November answers again, "Let's do eleven-thirty, and just bring your lovable self. I think we overdid it with the food ordering."

My best friend and I are so much alike when it comes to food.

"Great! Text me whether you get home or stop for the night. It's supposed to rain quite a bit here starting in the early evening."

"Will do! Love you!"

"Love you both!"

I exit the call and ask myself, *Do I love Rhys?*

For the way Rhys is to my most precious friend, how he loves her, yes, I absolutely do!

With house keys and a Watermelon Lip Smacker in my right hand, and a bottle of sauvignon blanc in my left, I knock on Asher's front door promptly at six.

He opens the door immediately as if he was standing nearby waiting for me.

When I originally thought him asking me to come over sounded like a date, I wiped the thought. Yet, as I was dressing to go to his apartment, I wondered why I was going to put on something 'nice' like I would for a casual date. Instead, I slipped my black off-the-shoulder sweatshirt I was wearing today back on my body.

Asher did change into jeans and a T-shirt, but I wouldn't expect him to stay in his kayak-wear.

I hand the bottle of chilled wine out to him. "I couldn't come over empty-handed, but I'm just realizing I have no idea if you drink alcohol."

He takes the bottle from me, looking at the label. "Thank you. I'll have a drink now and then. I like sauvignon blanc. Come in." His eyes are back on mine as he moves to the side to let me in.

The last time I was at his open front door, I was too preoccupied with him to see anything past him. I can't believe I missed this! The hallway is long. To the right are various doors leading to, probably, closets, laundry, a bedroom, but it's the left side that has me giddy. A long wall of nearly to the ceiling, well-organized but completely full, white bookshelves.

I barely hear the door click shut behind me. "Asher! This! I knew you were a reader, but I am in awe." I rest my hand on one of the shelves and scan the author names on the shelves at my eye level. Isaac Asimov. F. Scott Fitzgerald. Ernest Hemingway. Alice Walker. Douglas Adams. William Golding. Harper Lee. Frank Herbert. Toni Morrison. Kurt Vonnegut. Ray Bradbury. Alexandre Dumas. Jane Austen. Joseph Heller. Suzanne Collins. Mary Shelley. Paulo Coelho. And I think I might glimpse a few Dr. Seuss and Madeline L'Engle books on the top shelf.

There has to be over a thousand books, easy. I do notice they aren't shelved in a typical style like by genre. Only in a way that makes sense to Asher alone.

Curious, I ask, "How are your books arranged?"

When I look to him, he's retreating into himself, his eyes cast downward, shoulders curling in, arms crossing in front of his chest, the wine bottle still in his hand half covered by a bicep. I think I'm understanding now. This isn't him being shy, this is . . . *self-preservation?*

Before I know what I'm doing, I reach my free hand out and rest it gently on his forearm. An instinct to soothe.

He looks to my hand then back to me. Those soulful eyes behind eyeglasses appear darker than usual.

"I can see your books are in an order that means something to you, and if you don't want to tell me, I won't be offended." I can only hope my expression and body language he reads confirm my words.

"I should reorganize them according to genre and author, but I already know where each book is."

"Asher, it's your home. You can arrange your books however you want."

Asher exhales like he has been holding his breath. "Basically, the arrangement is the age I read them. I don't remember all the books I read when I was really young, but I did the best I could to buy what I do remember. There are years I read constantly, hiding out in a library until close, writing on a paper list what I read. Some years, I was too busy to read much."

There's a hint of hesitancy in his delivery, and I can't help but think there's more to this story. Perhaps he'll share more with me someday. I glance down the shelves. These books look new or barely touched. None look worn by time, nor boxed and moved from home to home.

When I speak, I sound throaty, like a plethora of emotion is crowded together, but I have no idea why. "This is quite the collection. I can't believe you remember the exact order you read the books of your life." Finally, I turn to face Asher. "You're welcome to add the books of mine you read from the lobby library to your shelves."

He looks–no-assesses me. "Thank you. I'll replace the books from the library though. Let's get to dinner and *Empire now*."

"Let's." I resume my walk down the hallway. With the shelves, there isn't space for him to walk beside me, but he isn't far. Perhaps it's imaginary, but I think I can feel the warmth of his body.

The hallway opens to a clean kitchen that is the same look but larger than mine. There's a decent-sized dining area that's been converted to a reading area with a large comfy-looking, saddle brown leather chair and ottoman jutting out from the corner. A standing lamp with a stained-glass shade in stormy grays has been placed behind a round marquetry side table with a compass design on top. My eye catches on the lamp shade again; a raven in front of a full moon.

I smile at Asher. "You like Edgar Allan Poe."

His soft smile makes an appearance. "I do."

"I read Poe every October."

"Very fitting, but I tend to read him in the winter."

For a moment, I mull over the cold of winter night enhancing the tales. "I think I can see why."

"If I promise to let you investigate my apartment later, can we eat now? I really don't want you to eat cold Chinese food."

This makes me laugh and he looks . . . I don't know what this new expression is, but at least his smile is a tiny bit wider. And it's my new mission in life to keep chipping away at his defenses.

"Be careful what you offer me, Asher. I will leave no stone unturned."

He gestures to the living area and begins to step back to the kitchen. "Have a seat and I'll pour the wine. Feel free to get started."

As I make myself comfortable on a wide Mid-Century Modern tan leather sofa, I feel tiny. Of course, Asher would have a sofa this size to lay down on while watching TV. Then I see the spread of closed takeout boxes, plates, forks, and napkins. The plates are a stunning deep blue glazed ceramic. The napkins are black linen. Definitely not your normal bachelor fare, and I thought I was fancy.

Asher joins me on the couch and sets my wine glass to the top right of my plate.

He is becoming the most interesting of people and I need to know more.

"The plates are gorgeous," I gush.

"There's a significant pottery community in Buffalo. I bought a whole set of dishes from a nearby gallery."

"I'd love to see it sometime."

"We'll go."

He's so matter-of-fact; I know he means it. Like I'm a part of his life now and we do stuff together and he makes plans. And I feel an immense warmth in my chest because of who he is.

I look to all the cartons. "When I said, 'I'll eat it all,' I didn't think there would be this much food."

He makes a sound that I swear might have been a chuff and it makes me grin like the Cheshire Cat. I can feel it!

"I'm not going to hold you to eating everything tonight, Genevieve, but I do want you to try a bit of everything."

"That I can do."

He begins opening containers and telling me what's inside each, then passes them to me to serve myself, but I serve his plate in addition to mine. When he sees this, he does the same for some of the cartons until our plates are full enough. There are small bowls of sauces that he names. Chopsticks if I want. I place my napkin on my lap. He really thought of everything.

He picks up the remote control and cues *The Empire Strikes Back*. I lift my first forkful of shrimp with snow peas to my mouth as the opening crawl begins; I hum with pleasure.

Asher's fork stops halfway to his mouth, and he looks at me. And looks some more but says nothing.

"My God, Asher! This is incredible!"

I sample a bite of the beef with ginger and garlic. It's just as insanely good!

"Where is this restaurant? I need to add it to my contacts for delivery."

"They don't deliver here." Asher's fork makes its way to his mouth, and he takes his time chewing while looking at the TV screen, but I don't think he's reading the crawl.

I've never seen him chew this long when we had dinner at my place. "Why?"

He takes a quick sip of wine but keeps his eyes on the TV.

"Where are they located?" *Why is he being so weird?*

He blows out a breath and, finally, looks at me. "The restaurant is in Canada."

My fork clatters against my plate.

"You went to another country for our dinner?" Honestly, I know Canada is not that far, but I do know you have to use a passport to cross the border.

"This is the best Chinese restaurant I know of and I wanted you to try it." He sounds embarrassed. "It's not a big deal."

"It is a HUGE deal, Asher. You didn't have to do that. You could have picked someplace local or a different kind of food. I don't expect you to drive a billion miles for dinner."

He begins with, "You're-" then closes his mouth. He begins again at the end of a sigh. "Fort Erie is not that far away. We can drive there together the next time we want Chinese and dine in the restaurant. I think you would like the drive along the Niagara River. We can tour Old Fort Erie too."

"Okay." I say it quickly and turn to the TV in time to see Luke dragged by a wampa into an ice cave. It's all I can manage to say around my heart beating in my throat.

Asher Adams might be the kindest soul on planet Earth.

Asher

As Asher buttons his slate gray dress shirt, he wonders when the last time he wore it was. It's been a while since he's had to wear something nice. Thanksgiving, probably. Maybe a client meeting since then. It's not often that he's invited out; that would require knowing people, but Asher understands he's not a person to be noticed.

After the bottom shirt button is slipped through its matching hole, Asher glances at his reflection in the narrow full-length mirror on the back of his closet door, and the odd thought of 'would she like this shirt' enters his brain.

Chapter Eight

GENEVIEVE

Driving to November and Rhys' house in their suburban neighborhood is easy. I know these streets well enough because I stayed with them when I first arrived by airplane to Buffalo. I decided to ship my car instead of driving it across the country to save on wear and tear. I was also anxious to get to my new home. Riding as a passenger in November's sedan afforded me the opportunity to look at the new world around me. I've memorized these once-foreign streets from me to her quite well.

I park my car at the curb in front of a neighbor's house; looks like I am not the first to arrive even though I'm only a few minutes late. I scoop up the large, fragrant bouquet of spring flowers dotted with the hot pink roses November and I love so much, open the car door, and step out into the little sprinkles of rain. I hurry to close the door and jog in my shiny black rainboots to the front door. For me, it's not rainy enough for an umbrella, but if my hair gets too damp, it will be a frizz bomb. I come to a stop once I'm on their covered porch, then take a few deep breaths.

The only one I really know here is, of course, November. While Rhys was in Los Angeles to help November move, and when I was a guest in their home, I got to know enough of Rhys to understand how deeply he is in love with my friend and that he would never intentionally hurt her. Honestly, that's all I really needed to know at the time. Getting to know him as the man he is, that will come over time.

As for everyone else at this brunch, I've met November's sister-in-law, Alex, a few times in the past when she and her first husband, November's brother, Roman, would visit in LA. A couple years after Roman died, Alex brought their daughter, Plum, for a quick trip to LA and I joined them and November for a day at Disneyland. We all had a great time, but I only really know Alex through November. I've never met Alex's new husband, Mark, and there's a new member to their family, an infant boy named Tristan. According to November, Alex really loved Brad Pitt in *Legends of the Fall*.

Then there's Rhys' siblings who I have never met, just seen their cookie-cutter images in photos. All tall. All black-haired with identical sapphire blue eyes. All gorgeous. Again, what I know about them is purely through November and she loves them, so I don't see why I wouldn't love them. Other than that, I have no idea who else would be here that they consider family.

I take one last deep inhale, then exhale completely before turning the handle on the front door.

There's music and laughter and the screech of a happy baby coming from the kitchen. No one seems to be in the rooms in the front of the house, and I have a moment to hang my trench coat and place my rainboots in the closet by the front door. After sliding on magenta suede ballerina flats I pulled out of my tote, I walk past November's gorgeous library and feel that pang of envy in my gut. I could live in that room with that ornate fireplace and floor-to-ceiling bookcases carved with roses and vines to match and be happy for the remainder of my life.

I continue down the hall toward where I hear the commotion of a party. As I scan the family photographs hanging on the wall as I walk, November sees me before I see her.

"You're here!" she exclaims.

My beautiful friend wraps me in her arms before I have a chance to fully turn toward her. November's long, dark chocolate hair cascades past her shoulders. Her reddish-brown eyes sparkle, her cheeks naturally pink. She oozes happiness and I couldn't be happier to witness this special time in her life.

"Hey you!" I squeeze her before letting go to hand her the bouquet.

She buries her nose into the flowers and inhales and doesn't even lift her face when she speaks. "They are perfection. Our roses too."

I gently tug on a few strands of her hair. "You're going to suck the life out of them."

She pulls her face away and feigns exasperation by rolling her eyes at me. My friend is normally slightly taller than I am, but today she's wearing high heels and feels like a giant. She wraps her arm around my shoulders and slowly steers us toward the kitchen, all while uncharacteristically towering over me.

"Alex is excited to see you. She felt bad for not coming around when you were staying with us, but Plum was sick, then the baby caught what she had, then Mark, then Alex. Like dominos falling. By the way, Plum remembers you as my 'fun friend.'"

"I am your fun friend." I bump my hip into hers.

"And I'm excited for you to meet everyone else."

"Sounds like quite the party."

"We set up a table for brunch on the patio. The fireplace is lit out there and the space is pretty enclosed. Food and drinks are laid out on the indoor dining table. And everyone can mingle outside or in. Nothing crazy fancy."

"Well, I can't wait to hear all about your trip. Did you have the best time?" I ask right before we step into the kitchen. "By the way you're beaming, I can tell you did."

"I can honestly say, it was life-changing!" Her sigh emphasizes her contentment.

Before I have the chance to respond, my eyes zero in on two tall men standing together in conversation near the sliding glass door that leads to the patio. The black-haired man who has his back to me is currently doing the talking with animated hand movements to punctuate whatever point he's trying to make. The taller of the two is no longer paying attention, because all of his hazel-eyed attention is laser-focused on me.

"Asher?" I don't know if I say his name out loud or mouth it, but he hears me nonetheless. He leaves who I now recognize as Rhys' brother in the middle of whatever he is saying to come to me.

"Genevieve." Asher sounds equal portions baffled and pleased.

"How do you two know each other?" The confusion in November's question is what forces me to tear my eyes away from Asher.

"Asher and I are neighbors." The words stumble out of my mouth. "We live next door to each other. How do you know each other?" My right index finger motions between my old friend and my new friend.

Rhys appears behind November and wraps his arms

around her waist. "What's going on? You all have the strangest expressions on your faces."

"Genevieve and Asher are next-door neighbors," November replies. She twists to the right to look at her love. "You said Asher lived by the water, but this is wild."

Asher shakes his head as if to clear it. "To answer your question, I consult with Rhys' company, and I went to college with his brother, Gareth. How do you know Rhys and November?"

"Genevieve is my best friend from Los Angeles," November answers for me.

"Gen moved here to open a bookstore," Rhys adds.

My eyes shut. The cat's out of the bag, even though I would like that cat to have stayed inside a while longer. When I open my eyes, Asher has his arms folded across his chest and he is staring at me like I'm a Rubik's Cube he's trying to work out.

He's not wearing his eyeglasses today.

"I thought I heard my name over here," Gareth states as he joins the growing group.

"Gareth," Rhys addresses his brother. "This is Genevieve Torres."

"Ah! November's good friend." Gareth extends his right hand to me. "And a beautiful friend at that."

Rhys and Gareth are both extremely handsome men, in different ways. If I had to assign a fashion house each would model for, Rhys would be the masculine aesthetic of Dolce & Gabbana whereas Gareth would be the preppy pretty boy aesthetic of Ralph Lauren. But there would be no doubt to anyone that these two are brothers, Gareth being the younger of the two.

I take Gareth's offered hand to shake. "Nice to meet you, Gareth."

"Pleasure is entirely mine." Gareth smiles, sapphire eyes

shining bright with what looks like mischief as he holds my hand longer than necessary.

I sense Asher's stance shift more than I see it. And I know Gareth senses it too, because he actually turns his face to his friend.

"Well, isn't that interesting." Gareth chuckles, seemingly commenting to himself more than to anyone else. Finally, he releases my hand.

When I look to Asher, he's definitely glaring at Gareth, and I have yet to see such a harsh expression on his face before now.

"Hey! What's going on over here?" I hear the bright voice before I see the source pop up next to Gareth. "Hi! You must be Genevieve. I'm Carys."

I've seen the siblings in photos, but to see the three of them in close proximity, their physical likeness is stunning. And, damn, their gene pool is a fierce one!

"It's good to finally meet you, Carys." She's too far away to shake hands with. "November has told me many good things about you and your family."

"Likewise. And I love that we have another girl in our group. You, me, November, and Alex will have to get together at some point soon."

"Count me in!" Alex comes around Asher to give me a hug.

"Alex!" I hug her tight. "It's really good to see you! Where are your babies?"

She releases me. "Babes are all outside with the daddies."

Rhys pipes in. "Why don't we all go outside? The kitchen is starting to feel like clowns in a car."

Everyone agrees and begins to splinter off toward the sliding glass door. Except Asher, who hasn't moved a muscle. We stand and stare at each other. I don't know what to say. I don't know what he's waiting for me to say.

"You're here to open a bookstore."

I guess that's where he wants to begin.

"It's a big part of why I moved here."

"Why didn't you tell me? I am a fellow book lover." He sounds like a person who is the last to know a secret.

I sigh. "Asher, to tell you the truth, I didn't want to say anything about my plans because I'm having a hard time finding a location. I didn't want anyone to know just in case my dream goes up in flames."

Asher's expression softens as he unfolds his arms. "I understand. Can we talk about this later? I would love to hear more."

He looks achingly sincere, so I nod.

We both head toward the sliding glass door.

"And Genevieve?"

"Yes?"

"Don't give up. I think your bookstore would be something magnificent to see."

I could cry hearing the belief backing those words.

Brunch was delicious! Eggs Benedict with crab meat and asparagus on melt-in-your-mouth brioche. French-style melting potatoes. Lemon ricotta pancakes with blueberry compote. A beautifully displayed Niçoise salad on a platter. Vanilla yogurt parfaits with granola and raspberry coulis. St-Germain cocktails for the adults. Shirley Temple for Plum, who is sitting to my right, and Rhys to her right. From what I understand from November, Plum, and Rhys have become best buds.

For the casual crowd, the food sure is fancy.

I'm stuffed!

Asher is seated to my left at this long table prettily

dressed in the yellows, greens, and lavenders of the season. Carys sits across from me, stroller with her sweet sleeping baby girl, Róisín, situated between her and her husband, Gregory. It is crystal clear that this tiny girl has her father wrapped around all her fingers, the way he fusses over her. Carys' heart eyes are something to watch.

Gareth is seated beside his sister, across from Asher, and the twins have been engaging in nearly nonstop conversation with me, Gareth more than Carys. Honestly, their enthusiasm was making me feel exhausted until Asher caught Gareth's eye. Whatever nonverbal communication was going on between the two ended with Gareth laughing, but he ceased his grilling and turned to his right to speak with Rhys' assistant, Sophie, and her husband.

I take a moment to look around the table, at all the people who make up November's new life. She has created a good life for herself here, surrounded by good people. When I study my friend, chatting intimately with her man, all I see is pure love and happiness.

"Are you okay?" Asher leans in to, what I assume, make sure I hear his low tone words.

I turn to look at Asher as his eyes search my face for an answer.

"I'm not going to lie, I'm feeling kind of tired from all this newness," I whisper.

"We can leave anytime you want. I can drive you home, and we can pick up your car tomorrow."

"Thanks, but I'll be fine to drive. I wouldn't mind leaving in a little while, maybe after we help clean up."

I hear the scrape of chairs to my right and turn to see Rhys stand.

"May I have your attention for a minute?" he begins.

Conversation around the tables dies down as everyone

looks to their host dressed in a light blue dress shirt tucked into midnight blue trousers.

"Thank you all for coming to brunch today. November and I love hosting you, but I have to confess, there's a reason why we brought you together here instead of a restaurant."

Rhys holds out his hand to November to help her stand, and wraps an arm around her waist, holding her close.

My heart begins to race.

How did I not see this earlier?

November speaks next. "While we were in Yellowstone, Rhys did this!"

She lifts the back of her left hand in the air for everyone to see the large, sparkling rock on her ring finger.

Gleeful gasps, hoots, and hollers fill the air. Everyone raises their glasses in congratulations to their engagement. I'm up like lightning to pull November into a tight hug.

"Oh my God! Em! I'm so happy for you." My words and my eyes both are watery.

When we pull apart, I see her eyes are equally watery. "I am so happy. Life with Rhys makes me insanely happy."

I reach for her left hand to get a better look at the oval pink diamond ring. "Stunning. Absolutely stunning. I would expect nothing less for you, my friend."

Everyone is crowding in for their turn, and I need to relinquish November to the masses. It's a reminder it's not just the two of us anymore.

Before I step away, November stops me. "Do you have time for lunch tomorrow?"

"Of course."

"Let's meet at noon. I'll text you where later."

Before I can reply, Alex and Carys sandwich November in a hug. As I back away, as everyone gathers around my best friend and the love of her life, it hits me how much November's life has changed. We were two peas in a pod.

The seam split open and she popped out, but I'm still in here.

I turn to the dining table and begin to stack as many dirty dishes as I can carry to clear the table, keeping busy to ignore the ugly emotion slithering through my body, shame heating my cheeks. When I pick up the pile of plates to carry to the kitchen, I see Asher studying me as if he knows very well what I'm feeling.

I'm exhausted.

While everyone congratulated November and Rhys, Asher quickly and quietly helped me clear the dining table. It was Rhys who spotted us and told us that the catering staff would be by soon to clean up. We made the rounds of goodbyes with one more congratulations to the lovebirds before heading to the coat closet. November links arms with me as she walks us to the front door. After placing my flats into my tote bag and sliding into my rainboots, Asher holds my coat for me to slip my arms into.

November watches us, a quizzical scrunch to her brow. She gives Asher a quick hug, then a longer one to me.

"We'll talk tomorrow," she whispers in my ear.

I squeeze her in reply, then Asher and I exit.

"Are you still okay to drive?" Asher asks.

"Yeah, I only had one cocktail and drank water and coffee the rest of the time."

"I know, but you said you were tired and that was a while ago."

"One of the best things about Buffalo is, nothing is far away. It took me fifteen minutes to get here. I'm not that tired."

We continue to walk toward my car, and if I had been

paying attention when I arrived, I would have seen Asher's truck parked on the other side of the street.

"You said you haven't found a location for your bookstore. What exactly are you looking for?"

I sigh. "Can we talk about this tomorrow?"

"Of course, but can you give some pre-information?"

I have to smile at his contained excitement. "Everything I've seen so far has been either too small or too big. I want to include a coffee bar and plenty of seating for customers to read, work, chat. I want display tables for gift items. I'll need restrooms and a backroom for storage and employee space."

"I love the addition of a coffee bar." He pauses, jamming his hands into the front pockets of his black jeans as he walks. "I would love to hear all about your plans when you're feeling up to it."

"Sure." I try to keep the embarrassment out of my voice, but I hear it.

We walk the remainder of the way in pregnant silence.

The late afternoon sunrays are beginning to streak through the clouds, yet the smell of petrichor lingers in the air. During the month I have lived here, that particular fragrance has become so familiar. I love it. I want to have a candle made with that scent, title it something like, *Rainy Day Reading*. Blend it with a cedar or sandalwood note. A hint of vanilla reminiscent of old books.

"I can't believe we know the same people," Asher murmurs.

"Right?" I chime in. "I already thought you were good people, but now I know for sure."

"Same."

My driver's side door sensor activates and unlocks. Asher reaches for the handle before I can and opens the door for me.

"If you wait a minute, I'll follow you home."

"Asher, you don't need to do that."

"You do realize we're headed in the same direction."

His words ping inside me for some elusive reason. I nod. "You win."

He's about to close my door once I'm tucked in but halts. When I look up, there's a quietly pleased expression about him. It's a new-to-me Asher look to catalog. Almost playful.

"A bookstore."

I grin at the subtle lilt in his voice. "Yep."

Headed in the same direction.

Asher

Laying on his back like a starfish on his neatly made king-sized bed, Asher listens to Pearl Jam's "Black" through wireless earbuds connected to his cell phone. He stares at one point of the white ceiling and mentally searches his plan for holes like he's about to execute any elaborate firewall he creates. Yet, for Asher, this plan is far more important than his day job, and he needs to get this beyond right.

The chime of a text interrupts his thoughts.

The melody that only belongs to her.

Chapter Nine

GENEVIEVE

If I'd been asked to bring something to November and Rhys' engagement brunch yesterday, I would have baked my dark chocolate raspberry brownies, November's favorite. So, I took a chunk of time this morning and did just that: one pan for November and Rhys, if she doesn't hoard them for herself; and one pan that I split into one half for me and one half for Asher.

I think Asher might be working from home today, but I text him for confirmation before showing up at his front door. After receiving an immediate 'yes,' I swipe my lips with Tiki Tangerine Lip Smacker, hoist my tote bag onto my right shoulder, grab the brown craft bakery box off the kitchen counter, then head out my front door.

Asher is waiting for me, standing in his open doorway, wearing a black Henley, jeans, socks on his feet. To my delight, his eyeglasses have returned. He looks good in black. He looks good in glasses. I imagine the black-framed lenses to be small picture frames because his eyes are works of art.

Where did that come from?

I thrust the bakery box out toward Asher. "I baked brownies!"

His eyes dip down to the box. Actually, I think he's looking past the box to my dress. It rained half the night, but during the other half, the wind must have been working overtime to clear the sky. It's warm enough to wear a summer dress with a cardigan on top, so I chose my long magenta one with the petal pink roses and a cropped cardigan that's a close match to the roses.

Asher takes the box from my hand and peers through the cellophane window. "Are these all for me?"

"You have half a batch, and I have the other half. Dark chocolate raspberry. I made another batch for November and Rhys. I'm on my way to meet November for lunch, but I really wanted you to have these now, while they're still warm and gooey. You can always put them in the microwave to warm if you don't want to eat one now. And they taste really good with a scoop of ice cream on top-"

SHUT UP, GENEVIEVE!

"Thank you for sharing." He says it like my word vomit is the most interesting thing I've ever said. "This might be my lunch."

"Dessert as the main attraction is never a bad idea."

Asher licks his lips. "Definitely not a bad idea."

I'm begging my cheeks not to blush, because it feels like we're not talking about brownies, but I know we are. This is Asher! He has never once made me feel like he might be attracted to me. But I am feeling so warm under his gaze, I want to take off my cardigan. How would that look in this bizarre moment?

"I'd better head out. Enjoy the brownies."

Before I can fully turn away, Asher speaks.

"I was going to text you, but you beat me to it. Are you available after your lunch?"

"Nothing written in stone. Why? Do you want to watch *Return of the Jedi* tonight?

He leans slightly forward as if the mere mention of *Star Wars* is magnetic. It's not me; it's that he likes the idea. But I do clock that I am wearing four-inch espadrilles and he still towers over me.

"No. We can. After. If you're still up for it, but there is somewhere I want to show you."

I tilt my head to the right. "Where are we going?"

"Since you'll already be out, I'll text you the address and meet you there."

"Shady." My eyes narrow. "You sound shady keeping your cards close."

Is that a chuckle I hear?

It was low and quick, but it was real and wonderful to witness. I feel giddy, yet need to rein it in or he might feel self-conscious. I don't know. He's always so reserved. I think he's becoming more comfortable around me, but I don't want to scare him away.

"Don't keep November waiting. Text me when you're done and I'll send you the address. Have fun."

My eyes are still trained on him and that lighter expression is still on his face, but he's right; I need to leave.

"Will do," I say, giving him a little wave as I walk away.

I don't dare look back.

I am eight minutes late to meet November at Delaware Park. I didn't realize how long I delayed talking with Asher nor how long it would take me to drive the side streets. Mind you, it doesn't take long to drive anywhere here, but some streets can get car clogged as I have discovered during my retail space search. I have also noticed that my eyes have been trained to seek for-lease signs and I tend to slow down to investigate.

Still, I'm late, but November doesn't look annoyed. Once I step inside the restaurant, she rises from the bench she was seated on near the entry. She envelopes me in a hug and I feel only elation at having November all to myself for a couple hours. I missed her. And it feels so weird for us to be together here, both living in a city that is not Los Angeles.

November breaks the hug first. "Isn't it strange that we're here in Buffalo together? I was thinking about it during my drive to meet you. It's fantastic, but surreal."

"Em! I was just thinking the same thing!"

"Great minds think alike." She smiles wide.

We are seated outside at a two-top table next to the railing, providing not only a perfect lake view, but I can see across to where Asher and I visited the cherry blossom trees. From here, I no longer see the abundance of pink I did before. Lush green now dominates the scenery, but it's still picturesque.

"All the cherry blossoms are gone," I comment.

"Cherry blossoms? Here?" November's head cranes about trying to see something that I just told her are gone.

"They were over there." I point to the Buffalo History Museum. "Is this the restaurant Rhys brought you for your first date?"

A dreamy expression washes over my friend's pretty face. "We sat at this very table. And . . ." She leans toward the railing to look past me. ". . . we had our first kiss just past where the pavement begins to narrow."

I look over my shoulder to where she described. "This is a pretty special place for a first kiss. Rhys knows what he's all about."

She giggles the kind of sound that accompanies the electricity of love. True love pinging around your heart like an old school pinball machine lighting up every nerve ending.

"It was special. He's special. The trees were in their autumn era; the moment was spectacular."

We're interrupted by a college-aged food server who takes our drink order of two St-Germain cocktails, something we tend to order when November and I get together. When the young man leaves us, November continues.

"Wait. When were you here?"

I begin my menu perusal as I make the quick calculation in my head. "Almost two weeks ago. The whole scene was stunning. You need to make a point to see them next year."

"I will. How did you even know that cherry blossoms exist here?"

"Ooooo! Do you want to split the truffle fries?" Everything on the menu reads delicious, so I make a fast decision of a classic Caesar. "Asher told me. He was going to see them, and I tagged along. Did you know his hobby is photography?"

"Of course, truffle fries, silly rabbit," she teases. "Do you want to split the large Caesar?"

"Shrimp on the Caesar?" I ask.

"Perfect."

We both set our menus down just as our drinks arrive and November takes the lead in ordering our shared lunch. I take a moment to study her. She radiates happiness. She found the love of her life clear across the country. I guess things like this do happen and it couldn't have happened to a better person. Everyone deserves having their person.

Our food server is pleasant, but the lunch crowd is descending and he flees the table as soon as our order is complete. He's about to become crazy busy.

"I don't know much about Asher. I've had maybe a handful of conversations with him since we met at Morgan

Security last autumn. He's ultra-reserved, but ultra-nice. Rhys trusts him explicitly and that says a lot. So, you just hitched a ride with Asher?"

"Basically. I didn't even realize what I was doing until it was done, but he didn't seem to mind."

"What did you talk about? He's not the most talkative man alive."

"Not much then, but we've been talking more. I feel like he needs to be around someone for a while before he relaxes. I think each time we hang out together, it becomes easier."

November's eyes examine me a few beats before she speaks. "Are you dating Asher?"

"Em! No! He's my next-door neighbor." I don't like how that sounded, so I add, "He's become a friend. He's kind and respectful and likes *Star Wars* movies and my cooking. He's a reader. He's going to teach me how to kayak since our building has a slip. If I like it, I'm going to buy one, even though he has an extra kayak."

Her reddish-brown eyes, those red flecks more visible in the warm sunlight, assess me. "You really are hanging out. Sounds to me like I missed quite a bit since I've been away. Sounds like you like Asher."

I roll my eyes. "Do not make this more than it is, Em. It's easy to be around him. But he's not my type."

"Gen, answer me this." November folds her arms in front of her chest. "How is your so-called type working out for you?"

"Ouch."

"No ouch. This isn't an attack." She gently rests the palm of one hand over the back of one of mine. "This is me wanting someone special for you, someone worthy of you. Someone who will take good care of the great big heart of yours. I think you can agree, your type is no longer a type you should hang on to. Perhaps you need to take a look at something new the way you are with your career. Maybe it's not Asher, who, by the way, is pretty easy on the eyes-"

"Hey now! I'm sure Rhys would not want to hear those words out of your mouth," I joke because I want to get off this topic.

"He's already heard it, and no, he did not like it, but I smoothed that over." She grins at the memory. "Look, I know this isn't what you want to talk about right now. You're getting fidgety."

I stop playing with the edges of my white linen napkin.

She continues, "I'm glad you found a new friend in Asher. I really hated leaving you alone, but it looks like you've gotten to know Buffalo way more than I have lately. You're settling in and that makes me happy. I'm still buying lunch, though. I need to purge the little bits of lingering guilt."

That makes me laugh. "You can buy me lunch. After all, I did bring your favorite brownies."

For a heartbeat, I think her eyes might pop out of her head. She gives me greedy, grabby hand motions.

"Gimme!"

"After lunch."

"Would you give them to me now if I asked you to be my maid of honor?" she asks slyly.

This question freezes me. My eyes begin to prick, so my brain definitely processed that bit of information.

"Really?" My voice is barely above a whisper.

"Gen, you are so much more than a friend to me. You're part of my heart. You have been there for me in so many ways. I want you with me on one of the most important days of my life. Possibly the most important. So?"

"Absolutely fucking yes." My voice is tight and I have to

clear my throat as I raise my cocktail to toast. "To important days and the forever kind of love."

November's eyes are equally misty. "To forever friends."

Asher

Asher places his truck in park, turns off the ignition, then unbuckles his seatbelt. He runs his fingers through his hair before resting the back of his head against the leather seat. Staring at nothing in particular through the clean windshield, listening as "Creep" by Radiohead morphs to "Fade into You" by Mazzy Star and fills the cabin at low volume, he thinks of the plan. He knows he's about to reveal a part of himself that he doesn't share with most people, and he's not ready to throw that door wide open, but he can allow a crack in order for her to achieve something brilliant.

To be there for someone . . . To be helpful to someone as deserving as he believes her to be, stirs hope inside him for something more.

He thinks, 'Am I allowed more?'

Chapter Ten

GENEVIEVE

The address Asher texted to me is for a wide, six-story brick building not far from home, also next to the water, and like many of the buildings in this area, has been repurposed. Something old that's looking new again.

It was easy to spot Asher's truck parked at the curb and there's enough space behind for me to park. Easy to spot his long, jeans-clad legs exit first after his door opens followed by the rest of his body. He's at my door just as I unlock it and holds it open for me. I step out, and he makes sure the skirt of my dress clears the door before he closes it.

Always considerate.

"You made it," he states.

"GPS was pretty straightforward."

"Good."

"What is this place?" I shade my eyes with my hand as I look up to the top of the building and scan downward.

He slips his hands into his front pockets, a sign that he's not completely sure of something, but he tilts his head in that universal 'follow me' sign and we walk around my SUV to the sidewalk as he answers my question.

"It's multi-purpose. There are thirty apartments–all rented I believe. Gareth lives in one of the apartments on the penthouse level. Level two houses affordable art studios and offices to provide services and training to foster kids. There are also rentable spaces for anyone who needs a classroom or conference facility or other type of event. Tenant parking is secured underground, but there is plenty of parking all around."

Asher continues to lead me to a large, sturdy, wood door painted a beautiful hunter green with glass panes. There is one large window to the right of the door and a bank of the same windows to the door's left.

Display windows.

I can barely breathe.

Asher pulls a simple metal ring of two newly-etched brass keys from his front pocket and gives me a look I can't decipher in my hazy brain, but I do hear his words.

"The entire ground floor is made up of different sized retail spaces. This storefront and a couple smaller ones are still vacant. I asked the property manager for the keys."

Before I can say a word, Asher has the door opened, standing aside to let me in first. I cross the threshold.

The space is a blank canvas. Expansive. Higher than normal ceiling. Cement floor just waiting to be covered. Fresh drywall on most of the walls, but the entire wall to the left is exposed brick and I immediately know that's where I want my coffee bar.

Mine.

Yet I don't want to get ahead of myself. And I can't seem to look at Asher because if I do, I might crumble.

"Do you know the particulars? How long of a lease

commitment are they looking for? How much per square footage? How amenable are they to construction? Do they use their own contractor?"

"They're pretty flexible on the lease and price, of course, within reason. This area is still up and coming, therefore, the rent is inexpensive. It's more they're looking for the right fit for the building. All the retailers here have been carefully curated. The building doesn't have a coffee bar, which would benefit the tenants and the surrounding businesses. Even though the coffee bar is attached to a bookstore, it would still generate considerable revenue."

Finally, I look up to Asher. "An all-romance bookstore. I might not have shared that tidbit with you yet. But my decor plans have always been to be more . . . middle ground. The exposed brick works great for my vision."

Asher mulls over this new information, then nods. "I still think your bookstore is a good fit."

His words are a zing to my heart. *Is this space a real possibility?*

He continues, "You will need to work with the contractor utilized by property management. I guarantee the work is quality. You should see the apartments. There are some things you cannot change, like the color of the exterior door and trim—everything exterior needs to be look uniform."

"I understand that. What about the interior?"

He shrugs. "You're free to do pretty much anything you want as long as it doesn't cause damage to the bones of the space. The contractor will work with you every step of the way."

"You probably don't know this, but how soon can I look over a lease? Do you know how long it will take to meet with the contractor?"

"I told Ryan, the property manager, that if the space is a good fit, you would probably want to meet with him immediately. He's waiting in his office for us. I can take you there if you think it will work."

This is really happening!

I shake my head in hopes to shake away the tears, but my whole body is vibrating with equal portions relief and excitement. And when stress breaks for me, I shed tears. Asher steps in front of me and places his big hands on my shoulders, but all I can see is a blur.

"Genevieve, what's wrong? Is this not what you're looking for?"

The concern in his voice is layered. I know Asher enough to understand: one, he's disappointed he couldn't help me, and two, he can't stand to see me cry. He feels helpless because he thinks he made me sad, and he might not be able to fix this.

Before I know what I'm doing, I'm leaning forward to wrap my arms around his neck, thankful I'm wearing heels. I don't even care that I feel how his body turns rigid in surprise.

"You have no idea how relieved I feel, Asher." I speak against his shoulder. "You have no idea how I was about to change my plans because nothing was working. You! You came through for me. I have no idea how to repay you for this."

I feel his muscles relax. His arms tighten around my waist. A real hug. A spectacularly warm feeling hug in strong arms that smells like clean cotton and something woodsy and masculine. I want to capture the scent in a candle and name it, *Book Boyfriend Hug.*

"You don't have to do anything for me. I just want you to have your bookstore," he whispers close to my ear.

I pull away to look at Asher, immediately missing his

warmth in the cool air of my future shop. And by the slump of his shoulders and the fallen expression of his face, I think he's missing the hug too.

When was the last time he had a hug?

I'll examine that question later, because the quick answer is a very long time, and that notion is too heartbreaking to acknowledge now.

I place my hands on his strong, lean biceps and make sure I catch his eyes.

"Thank you, Asher. You may never know the extent of how your thoughtfulness has moved mountains for me. How you just made my dream one more step closer to reality. A mere 'thank you' is most definitely not enough."

"Knowing that I helped you . . ." His emphasis on 'you' warms me from the inside out. ". . . is more than enough."

I see him start to either lean toward me or a reach for me or perhaps both, but he halts abruptly as though he thought better of it. Instead, he begins to lead me back outside.

"I could name a coffee beverage after you. Or maybe your favorite baked good."

He shakes his head, but his faint smile has returned. "No, Genevieve. You don't need to do that."

I step out into the sunshine on this monumentally glorious day. Allow the breeze to dry any remaining wetness on my cheeks. Breathe deeply and feel the weight of the world fall away until my next battle.

"It's my store, Asher." I hear the deadbolt engage behind me. "I'll do what I wish."

The property management office is located on the second floor, directly across from the public access glass-walled elevator. Asher explains to me that there are separate elevators for the apartment levels to keep the living spaces private, and the penthouse level, where Gareth lives, has its own private elevator from a private parking area in the core of the retail level. I choose to take a slow walk up the gorgeous marble staircase that curves around the elevator shaft to admire the framed photos of Buffalo landscapes hung on the walls. Beautiful imagery; some locations I recognize, some I don't.

At the top of the staircase, we cross the marble-floored hallway to an office with glass walls and door. Although I don't see anyone on this floor, I do hear the faint sounds of business being conducted from behind closed doors, like walking an empty hallway at a high school in session.

Asher opens the glass door for me to pass through to a small lobby with what looks like a meticulously restored, vintage minimalist reception desk. From behind the desk, a very young, biracial woman with short, fantastically wild red hair, dark freckles against tan skin, and the largest blue eyes I think I've ever seen stands when she spots us.

"Hi, Asher." I can tell this girl is trying her best not to fidget, trying with all her might to not show how awkward she feels. "Nice to see you again."

She is so young. And by the way she can't seem to tear her eyes away, she is massively crushing on Asher. Honestly, I don't blame her; he's a good man to have a crush on.

"Hi, Lucy." Asher's tone is kind.

He places a gentle hand to the small of my back. It's the lightest touch yet feels weighty.

He continues, "I'd like you to meet Genevieve Torres. She will be leasing suite seven to open an all-romance bookstore with a coffee bar addition."

I wish Asher hadn't said that. *What if I'm not accepted?*

I extend my right hand to Lucy. I'm taller than she is in

my heels, but I would be shorter without. "Nice to meet you, Lucy."

"You too." Her handshake is friendly and firm. "Your business idea sounds great."

"I can only hope it's received well by the community. I have a multitude of plans for special events."

"Did I hear something about events?" asks the man emerging from around the partition wall exhibiting another framed photograph, this one of the building I'm currently standing in. "You must be Genevieve Torres. I'm Ryan Sinclair."

Ryan, with his dirty blond hair, warm moss green eyes, height, and thick muscles testing the limits of his shirt sleeves, looks like he stepped off the pages of a cowboy romance. I have to rein in a giggle, but I take it as a good sign that the property manager of the building I want to house my bookstore looks like how a MMC is described in many romance novels.

After shaking hands with me, Ryan gestures toward where he first appeared. "Let's step into my office and discuss suite seven."

Both Ryan and Asher allow me to walk ahead, and once I step into Ryan's office, I find much of the same design as the lobbies I've seen in this building.

"I have to say, I'm kind of in love with what I've seen so far of this building. The merging of old and new throughout works beautifully."

Ryan hand gestures an offer for me to sit in one of the caramel-colored leather guest chairs in front of his desk, before walking around to take his seat. "There are photographs hanging in a couple of the conference rooms on this floor that document the building's renovation. You see the state of the building now compared to the shambles it was before and it's difficult to reconcile this is the same place."

"Have you been working here from the beginning?" I ask as I sit. Asher takes the seat next to me but pushes the chair back a bit to accommodate his long legs.

"Oh, no, but I came on somewhere in the beginning of the middle when there was more to manage other than demolition, pipes and wires." He sets a large tablet in front of me and moves right along. "Asher told me you'd like to open a bookstore and coffee bar. Do you think suite seven will suit your needs?"

"I do, but I don't think Asher explained that this will be an all-romance bookstore." I glance at Asher, but he remains expressionless. I return my focus to Ryan. "Will that be an issue?"

He looks in the direction of Asher. Whatever he sees there seems to be what he's looking for. But when I look to Asher again, I still see nothing telling on his face. He does look at me this time and gives me a little nod that I interpret as encouragement.

"No, but I've known Asher a while and trust his instincts." Ryan rests his elbows on the desktop, links his fingers together, and leans slightly forward. "Your business could be a benefit to our community for various reasons. We're very careful in our selection process; it's why we don't advertise availability. We want our businesses to be a complement to each other, not competition. We also want businesses our tenants may appreciate. Even though your bookstore is one genre, you have a coffee bar where people can gather that is not a restaurant where tables need to be turned over."

"What other businesses occupy spaces?" I inquire.

"A French café that opens early for breakfast and closes after the late lunch crowd. A wine bar that also serves small plates. A full-service spa salon. An art gallery and shop exhibiting works by the artists that rent studio space in our building. A small candle shop that customizes scents. Two other small boutiques."

"I like the mix. I'm looking for a custom candle vendor, so that shop may be my first visit."

"I like your collaborative spirit." Ryan looks down to his tablet. He scrolls through with his right index finger until he finds what he's looking for. "We do have one hiring caveat that you may or may not be aware of. It's on page three, section one of the lease agreement"

"What's the caveat?" I ask as I locate the section in my tablet.

"We house a training facility for foster kids aging out of the system, as well as offer other resources. Your commitment would be to hire at least one of our participating kids." Ryan gestures to the reception area. "Lucy is currently holding one such position, learning office and people skills, that will help her build a resume. This is a temporary position for her as we rotate the kids through, but you would be required to provide one permanent position."

I mull over the problem and solution for a few seconds before commenting. "On the bookstore side of the business, I would prefer to hire employees who are passionate about reading romance novels, but I welcome setting aside a position or two on the coffee bar side."

Ryan nods. "That works. There is a section in the application you will need to complete with further information about this commitment."

"I love how you found your niche to serve the community. I'm getting even more excited over opening my store here." I continue to scroll through the document in the tablet and my eyes land on the price, which falls in the low end of my price range, actually, a dollar lower. "Is this the total monthly lease price or is it a misprint?"

Ryan laughs nervously. His eyes dart to Asher, then back to me. "It's why we don't advertise. We would be inundated with applications. You are still responsible for your utilities, insurance, and other expenses you may have. But we keep the rental cost low, because we do have the hiring clause and we know that if we don't charge an exorbitant amount of rent, the outcome is probably a better business offering more services and better quality. This is a benefit to our tenants who do pay for their upscale apartments. Our business model is working for the six months we have been fully operational."

"Especially Gareth," Asher comments.

Ryan chuckles. "Especially Gareth."

Gareth slipped my mind. That's why Asher seems to know everyone here and was able to vouch for me. I'm sure Asher is around quite a bit with his friend.

"I-" I'm not even sure what to say, but the craziest analogy comes to mind and the words spill out of my mouth before I can even think about it. "I've only been to Vegas a few times, but during one of those trips, I was waiting for my friend to join me outside the restroom. There was this large shark-themed slot machine and I thought it would be fun to see what it does. I threw a dollar's worth of quarters into the machine, and when all the little videos lined up in an indiscernible way, all the bells and whistles went off and I watched the dollar amount of what I won keep rising. One hundred. Two hundred. Three hundred. I watched the shark swim across the screen multiple times and the numbers kept rising even though I had no idea what I hit. I'm kind of feeling like that right now."

"How much did you end up winning?" Ryan grins wide, showing his pearly whites.

"Just under a thousand dollars."

Ryan whistles long and low. "That's an insane amount!"

"Lucky," Asher comments.

I turn my head to look at what I could interpret as his surprised face: raised eyebrows, eyes wide behind glass lenses, and dropped jaw. A new expression to catalog. More important, though, is the lucky feeling I have to know Asher Adams.

"Exactly."

Asher

After the meeting with Ryan concluded, Asher climbed into his truck and followed her SUV home. He made a quick call to Ryan, thanking him for his help, then turned on music and listened to "The Ghost in You" by The Psychedelic Furs the remainder of the ride.

Later, after eating the dinner she prepared for them, Asher sat with her on the velvet sofa she says she loves so much watching Return of the Jedi and snacking on Red Vines. He didn't care she was more interested in reviewing the lease contract on her laptop. Nor did he care when she would pause the movie whenever she needed to talk some idea through. Even though he's seen this movie nearly a hundred times, it doesn't matter if this were the first: Asher would rather watch her, discover how her mind works, over anything.

Chapter Eleven

I signed and emailed the lease agreement this morning. After one last read through, I felt one hundred percent confident that this was not too good to be true. Lucy confirmed receipt via email and set an appointment between me and James Rutherford, the building's dedicated contractor, for Friday afternoon.

How will I celebrate this monumental first rung of my bookstore grand opening ladder?

A kayak lesson.

Asher mentioned the lesson before he left my apartment last night. I felt bad for not being present during our hang time, but I wanted to grasp every nuance of the contract before signing, basically ignoring the entire run time of *Return of the Jedi*–it's fine, not my favorite. Furthermore, I'm shocked Asher didn't up and leave after the fifth time I paused the movie to confirm my interpretation of a clause or to tell him about a new idea I had for the store.

First thing this morning, Asher knocks on my door to give me a hot pink dry bag (a color easy to spot if the bag falls in the lake, according to Asher) to hold anything I absolutely need to bring along, like sunscreen and my cell phone. I also pack a forty-ounce tumbler of water, two protein bars (just in case lunch doesn't see me through it), sunglasses, and my Fanta Grape Lip Smacker.

When I ask what I should wear, Asher replies, "Something you can easily move in, preferably lightweight, and sneakers you wouldn't mind getting wet. If you end up liking kayaking, we'll buy you a pair of water shoes."

He also texts me links to short YouTube videos about kayak safety, stretches to do before kayaking, and a beginner's tutorial. Asher is thorough.

The afternoon is warm, so I opt for a purple sports bra under a loose-fitting light gray tank top, denim cutoffs, and lilac and gray sneakers I should have retired a year ago. I force my curls into a long, thick braid which I snaked into the back of my sunshine yellow *Don't Be a Dick* cap.

Asher is also prompt, knocking on my front door at our agreed upon time of 2:00 p.m., giving both of us enough time to get work done. With dry bag in hand, I open my door, and give him a cheerful, "Hey!"

He doesn't say anything.

His eyes roam my body from my cap to my sneakers. Still nothing. He blinks as if to uncloud his vision, then, finally he gives me a monotone "Hey" back.

"What? Are my clothes not appropriate for kayaking? I can change." I look down at my legs. "Maybe I should cover my legs?"

"No!" He shakes his head. "I haven't seen . . . No, what you're wearing is fine."

I feel let down by the word 'fine' when he's referring to my appearance, but okay.

The door closes behind me when I step out, and I turn to lock it. When I turn back around, I catch Asher's pretty eyes dart up to my face.

Was he looking at my ass?

I can't blame him; I do have a nice round ass. Going hard on leg days-*worth it!*

"Kayaking awaits, Asher. Take me to the mini boats!" I start my sashay around the corner.

"They're not boats," he mumbles, but I hear him loud and clear and laugh all the way to the elevator.

Down in Asher's well-organized storage cage, although there isn't much to organize, he instructs me on how to carry my kayak. Well, his spare one that looks like it's never been used, and is the perfect match to my sports bra, a deep violet. I also notice it isn't as long as the one he uses. Who would have used this one? I have yet to see him have visitors, but I'm not always around.

"This is one of my favorite colors," I offer.

"I-" He glances at my bra strap and coughs. "Didn't you wear a dress this color when we went to see the cherry blossoms?"

"I think I did. You have a good memory."

I hoist my kayak onto my shoulder. It's not as heavy as I thought it would be. Asher stands close by to make sure I have a secure hold. When I give him a thumbs up with my free hand, he makes quick work of grabbing his gear and locking the gate.

I step outside the storage area first, right on the walkway along the river. That's when I realize I haven't been out here. Sure, I've seen this view from my balcony every day, but I have yet to be here on the ground. I feel the buzz of excitement knowing I'll be on that water soon.

Asher leads me to the kayak launch at the end of the property. He sets his kayak down on the dock before reaching for mine, but I take a step back.

"No, I want to learn how to do it all. I might love it

enough to keep borrowing your kayak whether you're with me or not."

He looks . . . proud of me?

"You are welcome to use your, I mean, *the* kayak anytime. I could install a rack in your storage unit to hang it."

"My unit is quite stuffed with Halloween and Christmas decorations, some items for the bookstore, and other things I couldn't part with, but won't fit in my apartment."

"Then I'll give you a spare key to mine."

"Are you sure?"

"Are you saying you shouldn't be trusted?" he mocks.

I feign shock. "Wow! Did Asher just kid me?"

"Don't you want to put down your kayak? Or are you okay with an extra forty-some pounds hanging on your shoulder?"

Sooooooo glad I lift weights.

"Show me what to do, teacher."

I spot the movement of his Adam's apple before he turns away to pick up his kayak again and recall how flirty I just sounded.

"Did you stretch?" he asks.

"I did." I check my tone.

"Good. I'm going to get in first, so you can watch me."

"Okay."

He sets his kayak on the launch, then notches his paddle in the grooves to use as a handle to step inside the kayak.

"Place your dry bag in first and secure it in the net. Outside leg in first, inside leg, then take a seat." He demonstrates each step as he says it. "Once you're settled, move your paddle notch-to-notch to pull your kayak down the slope. You might want to lean back a little when the nose hits the water. Go ahead and set you kayak on the launch."

As I situate my kayak, I hear the slap of choppy waves

hit the dock as the full weight of his kayak disturbs the water. I notch my paddle and follow the steps Asher just showed me. I'm a little wobbly, but I'm seated in no time.

"Good job," he says.

I almost thought I would hear a 'good girl' come out of his mouth, and I honestly don't know what I would do if he did. I wonder what that would sound like in his low, gravelly voice.

I'm thinking all kinds of thoughts today.

Notch after notch I pull myself down the gradual slope. When the bottom hits water, I'm reminded of the buoyant feel of the boat launch at the beginning of the Pirates of the Caribbean ride. This is so new to me, way out of my comfort zone. I'm thrilled to pieces that, one, I haven't fallen off, even though I haven't done much yet, and two, I have this amazing new friend that I feel I can trust and count on who looks out for my best interest.

Asher comes alongside my kayak and I take a good look at him in the bright sunshine. He's wearing contacts today and I decide I like both looks equally. He is very easy on the eyes, a quiet kind of handsome. Beautiful. A strong jaw with a little stubble today. Perfectly defined lips. The type of hazel eyes that seem to change their dominate color depending on the light. His floppy brown hair that he can hide behind when needed, hair that looks soft to the touch. Yes, extremely easy on the eyes, but I think what I like the most is that soft, good heart inside that rower's chest.

I snap out of my musing when Asher continues his instruction.

"This is a wide point to the river, so we will hang out here while I teach you how to use your paddle. When you feel comfortable enough, we'll go a little way upriver, but I don't want to exhaust your muscles. We can go farther each time we come out."

"Got it." I say without looking at him.

"I know I said you can use the kayak whenever you want, but I would like to be with you for the next few excursions just to be safe."

"No worries. I completely agree." I glance his way before peering over the side of my kayak. "How deep is the water here?"

"Twenty-two feet at its deepest."

"I've never been on water that deep." I chew my lower lip in the swallow of apprehension.

Asher reaches a hand out to my face but changes his mind and rests it on my closest hand.

"That's why we're wearing lifejackets. You will be completely fine. I promise to keep you safe." His voice is so earnest.

I release my lip from my teeth and feel relief wash over my skin, seeping into my muscles, because I know Asher will keep me safe, if it's the last thing he does on this planet. He's just that kind of man. The best kind of man.

Am I in trouble here?

I think I am.

Asher

Two days shouldn't be anything, but after the kayaking lesson, seeing her in those shorts, seeing all that smooth skin on display, the shape of her, the way the light reflecting off the water made her golden-brown eyes sparkle more than usual . . . Asher is wallowing in the absence of her, listening to "Dying" by Hole on repeat through his black headphones as he lays on his couch in the dark of night, unable to sleep.

This is how he sees this playing out: he can remain closed off and run the risk of losing her or open himself up and run the risk of losing her.

He speaks into the void. "Because no one ever really wants to know me."

Chapter Twelve

GENEVIEVE

Two days away from Asher hasn't made the confusing thoughts and feelings I had while kayaking with him any clearer. I make an excuse, so he won't think I'm avoiding him. I claim that I need to hunker down and solidify my bookstore aesthetic (long ago locked in) before Friday. He did ask to come along to my contractor meeting to be an extra set of eyes and ears, which I accepted, and he chauffeured me to the appointment.

I don't know what I expected of the contractor, but it was not this gorgeous, confident female with the messy honey blonde bun on top of her head, dark chocolate brown eyes, a full pout, and an upbeat attitude. Yes, folks, James Rutherford is a woman. I'm thrilled that, you know, girl power and all. Not so thrilled that she seems very well acquainted with Asher, and James is not shy about sharing.

"Asher was a great help with sourcing the ballistic glass windows and doors for the lower levels, and he drafted all the wiring schematics for the building. But, of course he did, he has a double major in computer science and engineering at Stanford, then went on to collect his MBA. Did you know he graduated from high school two years early?"

And . . .

"We can locate vintage oak bars for you that will look similar to the pictures you provided. A long one for the coffee bar and a shorter one for the cashier area. When we do, Asher will refinish them. Did you know he refinished all the vintage pieces you see around the building?"

And . . .

"Did you know all the photographs hanging on the walls in the common areas were taken by Asher? He's so talented."

And the real kicker . . .

"Yeah, Lucy is great! I love that all the businesses are required to hire kids from Perseverance . . . Oh, you didn't know Asher is the founder of the organization?

Yeah, I did not know.

Although it felt good to get the ball rolling on the bookstore build-out, I should have left the meeting riding an extreme high. Instead, I felt like the lesser of two fighters in the ring getting pummeled by information about my friend that I should know. Instead, I left the meeting with the understanding that this relationship is only superficial, and shallow has never been my cup of tea.

Talk about a mindfuck.

Logically, I know I've only known Asher for three weeks and I need to give myself a break for not asking the right questions. Emotionally, I feel like we're longtime, close friends, and I should know all the details. Yet we're both being standoffish in our own ways.

I know I can do better.

After saying goodbye to James on the sidewalk, Asher reads a text while we walk to his truck parked at the curb.

"Gareth stopped by my apartment on a whim and will wait for us to return. I texted we're on our way home."

"Is he sitting in his car?" I peel a curl from my cheek that a gust of wind plastered there.

"No, I gave him a key to my apartment a few years ago, against my better judgement."

"It's a good idea to have someone you trust have a spare. November has my only spare."

He opens the passenger side door for me, and I step up into the seat with Asher's hand assist.

"He wants to have drinks."

"We can watch *The Force Awakens* another time. I'll spend the evening working on next steps for the bookstore."

He rests an arm on top of the door. The sleeve of his white T-shirt slips back to expose more lean, corded muscle, and I feel the ghost of how his arms felt around me when I hugged him that one and only time.

"Will you please have drinks with us? I would really like you to be there. It'll be one drink because Gareth has a date later."

The flecks of golden amber in his eyes shimmer in the late afternoon sunlight, emphasizing the pleading of his gaze.

Can't say no to that.

"Okay."

When we arrive at Asher's apartment, we see Gareth has made himself at home on the sofa, simultaneously flipping channels with the remote in one hand and scrolling through his cell phone with the other.

"I'm bored," he states without looking up and without a greeting. "Let's go out."

"Why don't we open a bottle of wine here?" Asher counters.

"I'm in the mood for high-key, not low-key." Gareth, wearing a sky-blue dress shirt tucked into navy tailored pants like he arrived straight from work, clicks the TV off, then stands to face us. "Humor me."

In his black Mercedes S-Class, Gareth drives us to a local brewery that, frankly, we could have walked to. I've passed by multiple times and have been meaning to ask Asher if he wants to try it out with me because I'm not sure he has.

At the bar, I stand between my two tall companions and order a Paloma. Gareth asks the bartender what on tap he recommends, and after the bartender asks a few questions I don't fully understand because I've never been a beer drinker, Asher and Gareth agree to try the New England Style IPA. None of us have ever tried fried pickles, so Gareth places an order of those.

"Asher told me about your all-romance bookstore and coffee bar you're opening in my building."

"Are you the owner of the building?" It makes sense that Gareth would own it. He lives in the penthouse, but that doesn't necessarily constitute ownership.

"No, I don't own the building. With the amount of rent I pay; I might as well own it." Gareth glances to his friend, then back to me. "When do you anticipate opening? I need a place to grab my morning cappuccino, and your shop is very convenient."

"Very. If all goes well, I'm hoping to open mid-summer. I should be able to settle on a date by the end of June."

"Why all-romance?" he inquires.

"It's always been a dream of mine to own a bookstore and I'm passionate about reading romance." I offer up the simple answer.

"And what will the name of the store be?"

"Mine." Saying the name always brings a smile to my face.

"Mine?" He cocks his head to the right. "Why?"

It's obvious Gareth doesn't read romance, so I summarize the why. "Mine is known to be a romance microtrope. It's a point in the story where the author might have one of the main characters say it to their love interest as a possessive declaration to stir emotion in the reader."

"Mine." He ponders the word. "I look forward to your opening day."

The bartender, built like a firefighter, returns with all three beverages and sets them down in a neat row. "Pickles will be out soon."

"Thank you," I reply.

He gives me a nod before moving on to another group of customers at the now-full bar.

Gareth picks up his glass, sniffs the golden liquid, then takes a sip before nodding his approval. "This is quite good. You're not a beer drinker?"

"It's not my preferred alcoholic beverage."

"If you like Palomas, you might enjoy this IPA. Would you like to try a sip?"

I shrug. "Sure."

Before Gareth has a chance to slide his glass to me, Asher moves his body so close to my side I can feel the heat his body generates. He places his glass in front of me.

"Try mine. I haven't taken a drink yet." There might be a little tension in his tone, but I could be imagining it. When I catch the eyebrow raise and smirk Gareth throws Asher's way, maybe not.

I take Asher's glass in hand, and say before I take a sip, "I don't think Gareth has cooties, but okay." The beer is pleasantly citrusy. "Not bad, but I'll stick with my Paloma. Thank you."

When I give Asher a smile, I can feel him relax. He places a hand to the small of my back-not as lightly as he has before–and Gareth clocks the movement.

"I'll be right back," Asher states, before heading toward where I think the restrooms might be.

When I turn back to Gareth, his eyes seem to be assessing me as he takes a good swallow of his beer. I take this moment to take a satisfying drink from my glass.

"November told me you are good people. Loyal. Trustworthy. Kind. Determined."

"She's my best friend, basically my sister, and the sweetest person I know."

A food server arrives with our plate of pickles, forks, and napkins. She asks if we need anything else, but Gareth declines. I thought he might flirt with her, but I'm surprised he doesn't. Perhaps there is more to him than I originally thought.

He finishes another swallow of beer before speaking again as he swirls the remaining liquid around in the glass.

"Asher doesn't have friends. Well, I'm his only friend. He does know people; he knows my brother and sister well enough, but I'm the only one he really talks to." He places the glass down on the dark wood bar top before returning his gaze to me. "That trust was hard won over years. I earned his friendship, but I knew my effort would be worthwhile. There is no one more loyal than Asher, except Rhys." He gives me a knowing smile; it's a quality I want in a man for November. "It's been many years since Asher allowed someone new into his life. The jury is still out, but I think you–"

My eyes catch on Asher returning to join us, and Gareth understands he doesn't need to turn around to know. As much as I want him to complete his thought, I know he won't. I do understand that regardless of this façade Gareth puts on, he is a good friend to Asher.

"Did I miss anything?" Asher asks.

"Pickles." I slide the white plate in his direction. "We were about to give them a taste."

They're not bad.

Asher and I decide to order double-stack smash burgers and sweet potato fries to go and walk home to resume our movie night. Gareth grins hearing how we've been watching the *Star Wars* movies together. His family trademark sapphire blue eyes widen in a pleased, cat got the canary way. He retrieves his black leather wallet from his back pocket, pulls out a one-hundred-dollar bill, and sets it on the bar between me and Asher as he begins his departure.

"Dinner's on me. Enjoy." Not waiting for a thank you or a goodbye, Gareth exits the brewery.

"That's pretty nice of him," I comment.

"Yes. Or it was his turn to buy anyway."

I giggle.

After our tab is paid, Asher tells the bartender to keep the change. (A forty-dollar tip on a sixty-dollar bill. Nice!) Asher carries our bag of food by the handle as we set off toward home.

I know I'm car addicted when it feels weird to be on a walk—a habit I need to change. We walk in silence the first minute or so, the sounds from the brewery fading behind us. Since we left the contractor meeting, I have been needing to get some things off my chest.

I look up to where the sun is already making its descent, then take in my surroundings. This is my neighborhood and it's most interesting with a smattering of houses and buildings that look like I've stepped back in time. A small park with a couple baseball diamonds. My apartment building in the distance.

"I've learned more details about you today than I have in the three weeks I've known you," I begin. My eyes focus on the cement sidewalk, my ears on my careful tone and the sound of our sneakered footsteps. "I understand you're the type of person who prefers to keep your cards close to the chest, but I'm feeling . . ." *What am I feeling?* ". . . left out of the loop. You watched me admire your photographs on the wall. When Ryan and I discussed the Perseverance Clause, you said nothing. Were you going to keep quiet about all the work you put into that building? All the work you will be putting into my store?"

I wait several seconds for a reply, but I remain patient because I understand it's difficult for Asher to talk about himself.

"I'm not sure how much I planned to share with you. I knew I would have to come clean eventually, but I didn't know how. Then James outed me which was never my intention."

Asher stops walking, gently catching my wrist with his long fingers to stop me too. When I look up to him, there is a swirl of emotions in his eyes.

He continues, "I did want all that information to be given to you by me in my own time. I am deeply sorry. If I hurt you, please know, it was not intentional. I don't have many close people in my life, and you are quickly becoming important to me. I don't ever want to hurt you."

My heart is the trill of a snare drum as Asher's words penetrate my flesh.

"Thank you." I swallow. "I appreciate your sincerity."

He releases my wrist, looking defeated. It's my turn to reach for him, but I lace my fingers with his, feeling how much larger his hand is compared to mine, feeling the roughness of the callouses from working with his hands. I give his hand a kind squeeze.

"You are becoming important to me too, Asher. I am so grateful to have met you."

My words settle on him, and he smiles! The biggest smile to date, big for Asher.

I'll get him there, in time.

When we resume our walk again, I gently release his hand.

"Genevieve?"

"Asher?"

"There's one more thing you should probably know about the building."

"What's that?"

He blows out a breath. "I own it."

I halt my steps and can't think of one word to speak. I think he just short-circuited my brain.

He threads the fingers of his free hand through his hair and holds it there as he continues, "I didn't tell you because the last thing I want is for you to think I am doing you a favor. I truly believe your business is a perfect fit for my building and when I think of tenant possible needs and wants, the coffee bar with its work and gathering space is an excellent retail addition. I know the all-romance bookstore is niche, but I think it will pull in another type of clientele revenue . . ."

Asher word vomit is a first.

I hold up one hand to signal I need him to stop speaking, and he clamps his mouth shut.

Everything I have learned in the last few hours whisks into my brain. I have to laugh, and I do. Asher looks absolutely wide-eyed perplexed, like a cartoon, and it makes me laugh harder.

I grab his hand and pull him along. "Asher, you can tell me about how you came to own a building another time. I'm hungry and overwhelmed with the excitement of today. I trust you and you know what else?"

"What?"

"I'm touched by your faith in me that this business will be successful. I really needed to hear that from someone other than November."

"I do believe you will be successful." Asher doesn't let go of my hand. Instead, he threads his fingers into mine, and it's his turn to give it a squeeze.

I have so many questions I want to ask, pieces I want to collect for the puzzle that is Asher Adams. For right now, I'll keep it easy.

"Are you free tomorrow?" I ask. "All day?"

"Sure. Is this about bookstore stuff?"

"No. Is it okay if I want to keep it under wraps until tomorrow?"

He eyes me with pretend suspicion. "That's fine. Is there anything I need to know?"

I give it a good think. "Come by my apartment at eight o'clock, and I'll feed you breakfast first. We need to leave by nine. I'll drive. And you might want to wear something very casual."

"I'm intrigued."

I can't wait for tomorrow!

Asher

Asher wakes up an hour earlier than usual in order to get a few things done before he heads over to her apartment. He makes himself a mug of coffee with a splash of half and half in the kitchen, then shuffles into his home office to sit at his desk and write work emails. He planned to go for a long bike ride this morning, but he can do that another day. Instead, he hits the tenant gym at the end of the hall, bookending his workout with The Cure's "Pictures of You" and Soundgarden's "Fell on Black Days" streaming through his wireless earbuds, all the while thinking about what he could possibly be doing with her today.

'Does it really matter?' he asks himself as he heads back to his apartment to take a shower.

No.

He's willing to do anything if it means spending time with her.

Chapter Thirteen

GENEVIEVE

Although still a mystery, I currently understand that Asher is many things, but one in particular is: detail-oriented. At eight o'clock sharp, he knocks on my front door wearing a charcoal gray T-shirt with jeans and well-loved gray Chucks. He followed my directions exactly. Bonus points: he made a yummy hum after his first big bite of breakfast, and that sound is a song to my soul.

We sit side by side at the counter and eat steamy hot breakfast burritos I prepared: eggs, potatoes, cheddar cheese, crispy bacon, and homemade salsa in a large flour tortilla. Hearty. We won't be able to stop to eat once we leave today's destination. That's okay. I have stir-fry veggies and chicken chopped, waiting in the refrigerator for when we return home. Interestingly, I know for sure that Asher will join me for an early dinner. And, I must say, I like having a willing dinner companion. Okay, not just anyone. His company is comfort. I never feel like I have to be anyone other than the real Genevieve.

A little after 9:00 a.m., with stainless travel tumblers of freshly-brewed coffee and just in case snacks, we are heading south on US-219 in my white SUV, making unforced small talk and enjoying the lush green and wildflower landscape pass by. I inquire about his work, but it's not quite something I can completely grasp. When he puts it in context with his role at Morgan Security, Rhys' security company, it gels. He's an independent contractor who gets called in to hack existing client security platforms, program something far superior, and engineer it into existence in an undetectable manner. Asher does a slew of other tasks within his vast skillset, but my understanding is: he's a STEM guy.

Is it weird that I kind of like Asher more hearing how shy he is talking about himself?

I worry my lower lip. I did tell myself I would do better in asking the right questions, so I decide to ask the hard question. Something that has been nagging at my brain, something I recently put together when talking with Gareth at the brewery. Something I put off asking at the time.

I release my lip to speak. "Perseverance. Foster kids." I know I'm holding my breath. "Is this something you can relate to? Is that why you founded the organization?"

An uncomfortable amount of seconds tick by, and I think I may have overstepped in this new relationship–new friendship. But . . .

"My grandmother raised me from infancy until her death. I was nearly nine years old when she died. There was no known family to take care of me; I spent time in foster homes until I emancipated at sixteen and graduated from high school." Asher never looks at me, just keeps looking straight ahead, and I'm almost positive he isn't seeing anything. "My grandmother encouraged me to read and to always do my best in everything. I was reading at high school level and skipped a couple grades in elementary school. She instilled in me the importance of education, of a good work ethic. Being independent. She was my champion . . . until she couldn't be."

He pauses, and I don't interject my thoughts or feelings because I think he may say more. Not that I could verbalize those thoughts and feelings because 'sad' doesn't encompass them.

"She knew she wouldn't be there for me." His voice is lower now, sludging through memories I may never know. "I'm lucky to have had her in my corner for as long as I did, but it wasn't enough."

And because I'm a glutton for punishment I guess, I ask, "What about your parents?"

"I'm not completely sure." He shrugs, still looking forward. "I was maybe a couple weeks old when my grandmother became my guardian. The hospital had to guess how old I was-"

"Wait. Guess?" My mind is fracturing, trying to remain composed while bracing myself for the bleak story to unfold.

Asher shifts in his seat and right as I'm about to say 'never mind,' he continues. "My mother gave birth to me where she was staying at the time. In an attempt to sell me on a 'don't do drugs' lifestyle, and me being born an addict, my grandmother told me what she knew of my birth circumstances, but it's vague. My mother overdosed who knows how many days after my birth. My official birthdate on the certificate is an educated guess. No father's name. Fortunately, my mother had a driver's license on her. Social Services was able to track down my grandmother in West Virginia. After all was said and done, the doctors told her I was lucky to be alive."

I know I'm getting the basic information, but I don't need Asher to tell me the gritty details. I'm already feeling the bite of shame for stirring up his dismal memories, but I need to know one more thing.

I steel myself against the sting of tears, because I don't deserve to cry. "What was your grandmother's name?"

"Audrey."

"Audrey," I repeat.

"She named me Asher."

Before I can think twice about it, I reach my right hand across the console to lace my fingers with his and give his hand a squeeze, the only comfort I am able to give while driving.

"It's a great name."

Asher doesn't look my way, doesn't say another word. But when I'm about to withdraw my hand from his, he gently folds his fingers in and keeps it.

We arrive at our destination with five minutes to spare. I park at the curb in front of a very pretty, white ranch-style home with black trim on what looks like a half-acre of well-maintained land bordered by thick woods.

I unbuckle my seatbelt, then angle my body to face Asher, whose hazel eyes scan the property for any indication to why we are here.

"Okay. So. After years of pestering my parents, they gifted me an Australian Shepard mix mutt for my tenth birthday. I named her Happy. She was truly my best friend for fourteen years. It took me a long time to heal from her death. I've been wanting another dog for a couple years now, but my apartment in Los Angeles didn't allow pets. I want this new dog to go with me to work, so I thought it best to get one now and train it before I open the bookstore."

"Are we here to pick up a dog?" Asher looks around the

property as if looking for my new puppy, bewilderment written all over his face.

"Yep!" I quickly open my door and jump outside, anxious to get to my new puppy pal.

Asher joins me on the sidewalk. He unlatches the white fence and allows me through first before following me and securing the latch.

"Have you ever had a pet?" I ask, as we walk up the paved path to the front door.

Asher looks straight ahead at the house. "No. There were never any pets at the houses I lived."

Right.

"Do you like dogs?" *I sure hope so.*

Asher still doesn't look at me, his expression oddly unreadable. "I do."

"Good. I'd hate for Bisou to annoy you when you come over."

"Bisou?"

"I thought it would be a cute name for my puppy."

He doesn't verbalize an answer, but I do catch his head nod as we approach the stairs to the wraparound porch.

The black front door with a large brass hunting dog doorknocker opens, revealing a woman in her late fifties with perfectly styled, golden-blonde hair and a wide, genuinely cheerful smile.

"Hi! You have to be Genevieve. I'm Hannah," she greets, stepping outside to give me a hug.

After several phone conversations over the past month, it's good to put a face to the name. I give her a quick hello hug. After we release each other, I gesture in Asher's direction.

"Hannah, this is my good friend, Asher."

Asher takes a step toward casually dressed Hannah and extends his right hand. "It's nice to meet you, Hannah."

"The pleasure is mine, Asher." Hannah enthusiastically shakes his hand, then waves for us to follow her back down the stairs after releasing it.

"Mama and puppies are in the dog playground. Playground is a much better word than dog run, isn't it? It's such a beautiful day, I thought we'd have our visit in there."

We round the house, larger than it looks from the street, to the expansive backyard dotted with leaf flush trees, grass coming back to life, two large sheds constructed to match the house, and the white-fenced dog run.

My heart speeds up when I spot movement of white and black through the fence slats.

Puppies!

"We currently have three puppies here out of a litter of seven. Four have already gone to their forever homes and one of the three here is already spoken for. Whichever one of the two remaining you bond with, you will be able to take home today."

"I thought you only had one left," I ask.

"I did, but they backed out yesterday for whatever reason. I don't ask."

Hannah opens the gate to the dog run and allows me and Asher entry. Three adult dogs of various muttness followed by three puppies come running to greet their guests. The adults aren't jumpers, but the puppies are, and they are roly-poly bundles of cuteness.

"Let me corral my two foster fail ladies into the house." Hannah rolls her eyes. "I think Mama is going to be another foster fail for me; she's too sweet to let go of. It'll just be you two, the puppies, and Lulu. Feel free to sit on the grass and let the puppies come to you. The white and beige puppy is the one that's reserved. I'll be back soon." Hannah latches the gate and talks to her two 'ladies' all the way back to the house.

Asher continues to stand near the gate as I first introduce myself to the mama and give her head and neck scratches as I take a seat on the grass.

"Oh my gosh! Aren't you the cutest little mama ever!" I speak baby talk to the mother of my future puppy. The puppies advance closer to their mama and turn into wiggle worms, climbing on their mother, climbing on and off my cross-legged lap, especially the little white fluffball with black floppy ears and black patches on her back.

I look over my shoulder to Asher who stands with his hands in his front pockets. He looks even taller than he is. His eyes have turned forest green in the shade of a maple tree, and they follow the movement of the dogs and me.

"Come sit with me, Asher," I coax.

He steps forward, so careful not to step on anyone, and sits cross-legged on the cool grass barely inches away from me. The dogs pretty much ignore him, basking in my attention and baby talk. Except the other black and white puppy approaches him, confident and curious. She steps her two white front paws on his calves and wags her little curl of a white tail. Asher goes impossibly still, his entire focus on this puppy with one black eye, but that doesn't deter the little one from ambling into his lap. I hold my precious puppy to my chest and watch Asher, another one of his expressions I can't recognize.

The puppy climbs her front paws up Asher's chest and softly whines. Asher slowly raises his right hand and gently strokes the fur on top of the puppy's head, who turns its snout toward his hand and starts licking his fingers. Finally, Asher picks up the puppy and holds it to his chest and whispers "Hi." As I watch the scene play out, my heart squeezes so tight, I feel it may pop.

Hannah returns and rests her hands on the gate. "Well, Miss Genevieve, looks like you found your little girl."

"I did." I feel my smile widen to restriction; my eyes teary as my Bisou wags her tail as if she knows she found her person too.

"Why don't you bring her in the house? We'll go through the release checklist and paperwork for you to sign. She's twelve weeks old. If you're prepared, you can take her home today."

"I have everything I need to take her home in the car and at home." I stand with Bisou still settled in my arms.

Asher isn't so quick to stand but does release the puppy back to her mother and whispers "Bye" just as quiet as the "Hi." Once indoors, he remains silent as Hannah and I complete our business together. I peek at Asher from time to time to see if he's okay, but he never looks my way as he listens to Hannah's explanations and instructions.

After all is said and done, Hannah walks us to the front door and hands me a small gift bag as a happy send-off. She tears up when saying goodbye to the sleepy puppy in my arms and I expect nothing less. I can't imagine fostering-it takes a big, strong heart to do what she does.

"Will you send me an email with a picture of Bisou in her new home?" she asks. "I like to keep record of all the success stories in a scrapbook."

"I will. Thank you for everything. I can tell the dogs that pass through your home, and your fails, are well loved."

Hannah wipes at a tear before it falls. "They're family."

After one last hug goodbye, Asher and I walk the way we came to my SUV, Asher still impossibly quiet.

Halfway down the path, I break the silence. "I have two bath towels in the back seat. We could wrap one around Bisou and you can hold her in your lap. She's tired from all the excitement and will probably sleep the entire ride home."

Asher abruptly halts. I stop and turn around to see

what's going on. He takes a long look at me, then Bisou, and I know what's going on in his head and heart.

I smile. "As I said, Asher, I have two towels in the car."

Asher turns around and jogs back to the house.

"Looks like your sister is coming home with you," I whisper to Bisou, who lazily wags her tail in two circles.

After almost an hour of completing paperwork, and because he is my next-door neighbor and Hannah has 'a good feeling,' Asher is now buckled into the passenger seat holding two sleeping puppies bundled in towels on his lap. I glance at him during our drive to the pet store where I shopped for Bisou's necessities. He holds the puppies protectively, barely taking his eyes off them when speaking with me. I would have to have a cold, dead heart not to feel enchanted.

A man holding puppies is always adorable, right? Nothing weird about how I'm feeling.

"I know becoming a dog dad was not on your bingo card today, but any ideas for a name?"

Asher looks down at his puppy nestled in his lap for a long moment before answering. "Jin Erso."

"Perfectly you, Asher." I can't help my giggle. "You know, when you tell people her name is Jin, they'll think you named her after alcohol."

"I don't care." He smiles and it's the first real smile I've seen on his face all day but quickly turns melancholy. "I wanted a dog when I was young and living with my grandmother. I didn't know it then, but I think she knew she wouldn't be around to help me look after a pet. As an adult, I didn't think a dog would-" He shrugs off the thought and turns his gaze to the puppy stretching to a sitting position to look at him as if she knows he's talking about her. "When Jin approached me, I knew she was mine. I couldn't leave her behind."

When he bends his neck to place a kiss to the top of Jin's head, there's that squeeze in my heart again, but add a lump in my throat to go with it.

I swallow before glancing at him. "Well, I think you're going to make a great dog dad."

Asher doesn't look up, but I think I see a slight blush bloom across his cheekbones.

Yes, he's going to be a truly great dad.

Asher

Not one minute of sleep came to Asher last night, but paranoia was plentiful. He tried reading until he realized he was just staring at the pages. He leaned against the headboard and attempted to work on his laptop, but he was unfocused. He even placed headphones on his ears to listen to music but immediately removed them when he couldn't hear anything beyond the music. All because of the crate beside his bed and the new tiny responsibility within. If Jin whined for him, needed him, he would loathe himself if he wasn't there for her or broke her trust.

As dawn breaks and he hears Jin stir in her crate for the twentieth time during the night, he thinks to himself, 'Still, best decision ever.'

Chapter Fourteen

GENEVIEVE

With getting Asher settled with his new fur baby and welcoming Bisou home, I forgot my standing invitation to the Morgan-Day Family Sunday Brunch. I text a selfie of my face smushed against Bisou's to November with:

> Hi Auntie Em! I'm Bisou-can't wait to
> meet you!

Instant reply:

OMG!!! You better not be kidding me! Is
she really yours?

> Yep! And I don't want to leave her alone
> so soon. Won't be attending brunch.

Can I stop by later to meet your cutie?

> I'll be home all day.

I'll stop by after brunch.

See you soon!

November is knocking on my front door in the exact number of minutes it would take to walk to her car after brunch, drive from Delaware Park to my apartment building, park, and take the elevator up.

I open the door and immediately thrust Bisou into her grabby violet manicured hands. November pulls Bisou into her chest and baby talks to my puppy.

"Hello there! Hello Bisou! Aren't you the most precious baby? You are just the sweetest puppy! My new baby niece. Hi! Oh, hi!"

No hello for me, but isn't that the way of dog versus human?

"How long have you had her?" November asks, her entire focus on the puppy basking in her attention.

I pause until November's eyes look my way. "I'm sorry. Are you asking me or Bisou?"

She steps inside my apartment, cradling Bisou like a baby, and lavishing pets to her little white puppy belly.

"Who knew your mommy is so jealous?" she coos to Bisou. "Yes, she is."

Bisou is a fan, but anyone who meets November is.

"I should start getting used to it." I snort as I close the door behind her. "Do you want something to drink?"

"No, thanks. I can only stay a little while. Rhys has a work trip, and I want to drive him to the airport." She makes her way to the living room, still cooing to Bisou.

"You could have come over after the airport."

"Rhys needs to pack, and I'll only distract him."

"You could leave him alone while he packs."

"No, no, no. Rhys seeks me out." She takes a seat on the sofa closest to the window, placing my love-bathing Bisou in her lap. "Rhys is metal to my magnet."

"And vice versa." My friend is not kidding me into believing she's not blooming under all her love's attention.

November smiles. "And vice versa."

"Oh!" The best idea pops into my head and I reach for my cell phone on the coffee table. "Let me text Asher to bring his puppy over."

> November is here and would love to meet Jin. Are you available?

"Asher adopted a puppy?" November's tone is bright with surprise. "That's quite a coincidence."

It takes a long moment for Asher to respond.

> Jin fell asleep on my chest and I don't want to move her yet. I'm sorry.

I mentally paint a picture of Asher laying on his couch, Jin tucked into a cute ball on his chest, right over his heart, and Asher not moving a muscle. Maybe he's reading the copy of *Under Loch and Key* by Lana Ferguson I saw on his side table yesterday.

He's really branching out in romance.

> No worries! Come over later for dinner.

> I will. Thank you.

"Aw! Jin found herself a good daddy. Wrapped him around her little toe bean. He's going to be such a helicopter parent." I chuckle while staring at my phone screen.

I think about Asher giving all the love he never received nor was able to give to his sweet little puppy. I think about Asher as a parent to a human child. Perhaps a little girl. I bet he'd be a spectacular girl dad. Maybe a little boy who would be a little mini version of him. A little boy just like Asher because why wouldn't the world want more men like him. More kindness and-

"What's going on in that pretty head of yours?"

November's voice shakes me present and I return my phone to the coffee table in a fumble clatter.

Yeah, Genevieve, what is going on?

"Um, Asher can't come over right now, so maybe you'll meet Jin during another visit."

"Asher named his dog after his favorite alcohol?" Her face scrunches at the thought.

I giggle at her sour face. "You know, I told Asher people would think that, but it's actually the name of the heroine in *Rogue One*."

"Anyway." November shakes her head. "Asher adopted a puppy the same time as you did."

"He came along with me to Ellicottville to pick up Bisou. Hannah, the foster mom, happened to have another puppy available that absolutely fell in love with Asher, and he could not leave her behind. It was too sweet a scene for words. So, we came home with two puppies."

"You're parenting together?" November's making a big statement but says it as a question.

"What?" My hand waves her off. "Bisou and Jin are sisters, and it's nice they get to spend time together since Asher and I live next door to each other."

"And you and Asher spend time together." Her expression is pointed.

The direction this conversation is shifting to makes my pores want to sweat. It's not that warm of a day, but the air in my apartment feels suddenly stuffy.

"We do spend time together. We're friends." My voice is small because I'm beginning to not believe my own words.

November pats the sofa cushion next to her for me to sit

down, and when I comply, she gathers the now-sleepy Bisou in her hands and places her in my lap.

"I think you need some puppy love energy to get you through my next question, my friend."

Bisou curls into a ball on my lap. My fingers get lost in the black fur along her back and I don't respond to November's words.

She continues, gently. "Do you like Asher? And I don't mean as your nice next-door neighbor turned friend. Do you have deeper feelings for Asher? And before you answer, there is little you can hide from me. I saw your face when you were texting with him."

That's the thing with someone who knows you too well: through time and care they know you from that place of love.

"I think . . ." I'm holding my breath after the exhale and know I won't be able to take a fresh inhale until I get this out. "I think I do."

I take the inhale as I keep my focus on how pretty my fuchsia fingernails look against Bisou's black fur. If I look at November, she will see how true my words are. How I have been slowly thinking about Asher in a 'more' kind of way.

More time together.

More getting to know each other.

More touching.

More blending of lives.

November places a warm hand on top of mine, stilling my hand on the sound asleep puppy.

"I think you do too," she quietly states. "It's not a bad thing."

I finally look up to see my best friend beaming at me.

"It's an inconvenient thing," I say slightly above a whisper.

"Take it from someone who knows, love has its own

timeline." She blows out a breath with her chuckle as she leans back against the sofa. "I never expected Rhys to show up in my life. I never expected Rhys to keep showing up for me in so many ways since, making me fall more in love with him on the daily. But do you know what the most important thing was that I did?"

"Tell me."

"I allowed my heart to open up to Rhys."

"Easy breezy." I roll my eyes.

"No, but I felt our connection, and that Rhys is a good man. I made a decision and it was the best I've made in a long time. Maybe the best life decision I've ever made. And I do remember my best friend encouraging me through it all." She smiles wide, bright as the sun shining. "Love is stunning, Gen."

"I remember." There's a radiance to November that wasn't there pre-Rhys. The love glow up is real and she is living proof. "And you wear that love well."

November drums her elegant fingers on the navy velvet of the seat cushion.

"You could too, my lovely."

"I could too, my lovely." I sigh.

I swallow down the lump that was forming in throat, then notice I have raised a hand over my breastbone. Right over my wildly beating, traitorous, opening heart.

Asher

He has no idea what he's walking into, but when she opens the door to let him in, Asher immediately feels and sees her anxiety. That makes him see red.

Chapter Fifteen

GENEVIEVE

I know I need to get up and do something productive with the waning afternoon. November left well over an hour ago and her words still have me paralyzed as I turn our talk over and over in my head. I'm not going to backpedal what I said about having feelings for Asher. I have more feelings for Asher than I know how to deal with. Now that I've admitted it to November, I'm wondering if I should admit it to the man himself.

My cell phone vibrates against the wood of the coffee table, signaling a text. I reach forward and angle the screen to read the text from my second oldest brother, André.

> Hey hermanita! I'm in town. I'd love to
> have dinner with you.

"Fuck! Fuck! Fuck! Fuck!" I exclaim as I shoot to my feet and begin to pace the length of the sofa. "Fuck!"

Bisou looks up from her chew toy, bewildered by this new show of emotion and doesn't know how to respond. I give a couple rushed pets to her head, foist the toy back into her mouth, and it's like my outburst never happened for her.

"Sorry, little girl. Mom made a horrible mess that she has to clean up."

I take a couple deep breaths, then call André. The brother I'm supposed to be closest to yet haven't told I moved.

"Gen of the Eve! You could have texted if you're busy or not."

I hear my brother's smile and I know it's short-lived.

"An of the Dre!" I smile and I know it's short-lived. "I have some news to share and you are not going to be thrilled with me."

"No?"

Yep, short-lived.

"No."

He sighs. "What did you do?"

Here it goes . . .

I squeeze my eyes shut as if that's going to make this any easier.

"I don't live in Los Angeles anymore."

Dead. Silence.

I chew the inside of my cheek.

And more dead silence.

"André?"

"What do you mean you don't live in Los Angeles anymore?" His voice is monotone. "Where do you live?"

Oh, he is NOT going to like this at all.

I remain calm and clear in tone. "Buffalo, New York."

Why do I always feel ten years old around my brothers?

"What the fuck? When the fuck?"

"I moved mid-April."

There's a familiar wrap of knuckles against my front door, and I know it's Asher. As I listen for my brother's response and approach the entry hall, I wonder if I should answer the door. Does Asher really need to hear this conversation? I could shield him from my mistake. But I know November would say some shit like, "Opening your heart means letting the object of your affection see the real you."

"I can't-" André sputters. "I don't-You know, I think we need the rest of the family on this call. What time is it in France? Nine? Ten? Maman's awake."

I wrench open the door. Decision made.

"André, I will tell everyone myself. I'm sorry you had to find out this way and that's on me, but I needed to get my plan in order first."

Asher, dressed in blue jeans and a classic white tee, is holding a bright-eyed Jin like a football, leash hanging loose in his hand. Jin wiggles her hello in seeing me, and I put out my left hand for her to lick and receive pets. I look up to Asher and by the way he has furrowed his eyebrows, he already knows something isn't right.

I wave Asher to come inside.

"Yes, you will tell everyone yourself, and you're going to tell them now."

Before I can say another word, I hear André place me on hold while he calls Maman or whichever brother next.

Bisou rushes to greet Asher and her sister. Asher places Jin on the floor and lets the puppies chase each other around my apartment before he turns back to me.

He leans forward to meet my eyes. "Are you okay?"

His unwavering concern warms me in the center of my chest and I wonder a moment if hearing this family conversation will be too much for him. Yet I know in my gut that Asher is stronger than that. He's had to be strong his entire life.

I set my cell phone on speaker and place it on the edge of the kitchen counter where we are standing.

I exhale audibly. "My brother, André, called and I told him something that ticked him off, and now he's putting all the family on a conference call."

The phone line reopens and I can hear the group chatter of greetings and variations of 'What's going on?'

Asher's back straightens, returning to his full height. "I can leave and give you privacy."

"No, Asher, you should probably hear this."

Is that relief I see in his shoulders? Is he relieved I'm letting him stay?

"Gen, who are you talking to?" André probes. "Do I hear a man's voice?"

Merde!

"My friend, Asher, is here."

"Are you living with a man? Is this what the call is about?" Elias, five years older than I am, whines. Elias and I aren't very close. I don't think he ever got over losing baby of the family status when I came along.

"No, but I do have a new puppy named Bisou," I say in an attempt to lighten the mood.

"Tell me you're not trying to be funny right now," André chides.

"Bonjour, ma chérie."

Hearing my mother's voice is equal portions relief and a gut punch.

"Bonsoir, Maman!" I chime, then study the small tattoo etched on the inside of my left wrist: *Love you* written in my mother's handwriting. My guilt soars.

"Bisou is your dog's name?" Maman asks. "C'est mignon."

"I thought it was cute too."

Asher tenderly wraps a hand around my wrist and smooths over the letters with his thumb. My brown eyes meet his hazel. I see warmth and reassurance. I see 'I got you.' I feel it through my skin, through my blood, my muscle, and bone. Just like I hope he felt when I took his hand in mine during yesterday's car ride.

"Hola, Maman, Gen, Elias. André, we're all here. Can we speed this along? I sent Greta to have a mani/pedi and I'm alone with all the kids."

Diego is my eldest brother by ten years, married to a gorgeous woman with the sweetest temperament. They have four kids, and I'm not completely sure they're done.

"Sure," André begins. "Genevieve moved to Buffalo, New York. Is that fast enough for you?"

I hear background noise. The odd laugh and howl of children on Diego's line. Traffic sounds from whatever street André is currently on. The muffled laugh of Elias. And I'm sure they hear the squeaks of the toys the puppies are playing with.

"¿Que?" Diego questions slowly.

"Genevieve, c'est vrai?"

The disbelief in Maman's voice is a knife to the gut, but my eyes never leave Asher's. He doesn't flinch. Doesn't take his eyes from mine. Doesn't stop soothing my wrist. Regardless of my current predicament, I feel strong.

"It's true, Maman. I left my job and moved here in mid-April. I'm so sorry I didn't say anything when we spoke last week. I feel terrible, but I wasn't ready to tell you, to tell any of you. Brace yourselves-I'm opening a libreria con café."

I think I heard my father's ashes stir somewhere on the wind.

I glance at my dad's *Love you* on my right wrist.

Sorry, Papá.

"I know you like to read, but this is so far out in left field," Diego states.

Now, that has my back up. They have been dismissing

me and my dream for years even when I've been very vocal about it.

"It's not. If you paid attention, you would know this is something I've wanted to do for a long time. And-"

André butts in. "To go from a high paying job to something that will probably crap out in less than a year is insane!"

My eyes dart to Asher's, and there is a brand-new expression that I can easily interpret: flaming anger. His lips are parting to speak, but I don't want his first interaction with my family to be angry words. My hand reaches up to cup his jaw, to draw his attention to me, and the feel of his warm, unshaven skin against my palm grounds me. By the way his anger dissipates, it grounds him too. His need to protect me bolsters me.

Calmer, I plead my case, ignoring my brother's lack of faith in me, understanding he's speaking from anger. "I'm grateful for that job, truly, because it allowed me to build my nest egg for this opportunity. Moving to Buffalo is more cost effective to open my bookstore. Asher found me a retail space at a great price. Work is already underway, and I'm hoping, if all goes well, to open on June twentieth." I say this all to Asher, to tell him my truth as economically as possible. "To be fair, I know there are no guarantees, but I have to try. Opening this shop was inevitable; trying to live up to your expectations just delayed it. I have a support system here. I have November and Rhys, and I have Ash-"

"This really is a stupid move," Elias interrupts. "I can't believe you left LA."

"Elias, YOU left LA," I hiss. "And may I remind the rest of you? You all left LA."

They all left me, expecting me to stay put.

"Gen, you're not stupid, but this is not like you," Diego adds.

"I know I'm not stup-"

"Not like you at all. Maman, tell her," André urges.

"Maman." I hear the tiniest bit of desperation for someone to give me just a little grace.

Then Maman quietly states, "Non, this is not like you, ma chérie . . ."

This is why I waited. Not one of the people who are supposed to want the best for me supports my dream.

And there, there is the angry, hurt, hot mess blur of tears, making everything look like I'm underwater.

"You know . . ." I keep my voice as steady as I can. "Je t'aime . . . pero . . ." There is nothing more to say without going round and round again. So, I do something I have never done: hang up on my family. And power down my cell phone completely.

No more for today.

Without missing a stroke to my wrist, with his other hand, Asher gently hooks a finger under my chin to raise my face to look at him. He wipes away the first big teardrop that spills onto my cheek with his thumb, and this simple, caring act triggers other tears to fall.

"I didn't want to come to the end of my life and have this one nagging regret," I explain in a watery voice. "I knew if I told my family beforehand, they would have talked me out of it, again. I kept doubting myself until I finally made the choice to do what's right for me."

None of my tears get far because Asher catches them all.

"What can I do?" he asks.

"I could really use a hug," I sob out.

Asher doesn't hesitate wrapping his long arms around my shoulders, pulling me into his chest that smells like the most soothing mix of clean cotton warmed by the sunshine and, now, salty water as I continue to quietly cry and soak his T-shirt.

When my stomach growls, loudly, I mumble, "And maybe a cheeseburger with fries."

The rumble of his chuckle against my cheek makes the corners of my mouth tip up, and I think he feels it.

"Do you want to take a walk to the brewery?" he offers.

"I could use some sun and fresh air." *I could also just stay in his arms like this.*

Asher cinches his arms a little tighter as if the idea of letting me go is not a good one.

"Did I hear you speaking words from three different languages?" he asks after a long pause.

"It's Franglish."

Asher

Regardless of the strife she's experiencing with her siblings, her mother; Asher heard the language they have created over decades and use with each other, the care her brothers have for their sister, even in their anger. A close family. A dynamic he has never known nor grieved since he was a child.

He doesn't want to, yet now can't seem to stop the thoughts and feelings that produce a hope he shouldn't have.

Chapter Sixteen

GENEVIEVE

Sunday was an early night. Exhausted by the family drama and the heavy dinner we ate after walking the puppies to and from the brewery, I took a quick shower, put on fresh pajamas, and was asleep in no time.

I woke up early Monday morning and got in a good workout and showered before breakfast on the balcony where I found Asher on his balcony eating a bowl of yogurt with berries and granola.

"So, Nessie is a dude and the whole thing is a family curse that only her magic can break," Asher says after taking a sip of coffee and holding up *Under Loch and Key* for me to see.

I would know what he was talking about even without seeing the book.

"And the love story between Keyanna and Lachlan?" I truly wonder what he will say.

"Magical!" He smirks.

I giggle. "Do you know what you'll read next?"

"What about that cowboy romance you were reading under the cherry blossom tree?"

"That's a good starting point. I'll knock on your door to give you the book before I head out today."

Asher takes a sip from his mug, swallows, then inquires, "How are you feeling today?"

"Wrung out." I pick up my own mug, the warm stoneware cupped between my palms, providing a tiny bit of comfort. "I turned my phone back on this morning but didn't read any of the texts. I know this isn't the last of this. Me hanging up on my family was a huge deal. My brothers can go fish, but I know I need to talk with Maman soon."

"Can I do anything for you?" Asher doesn't just sound sincere; he is sincere.

"Thank you, but I know this needed to break before putting it back together again. Me not telling them I was moving is my mistake, but my family needs to let me live my life." I'm about to take a bite of my avocado toast when I remember something. "Oh yeah! James texted that she located the vintage bar I wanted, and it will be delivered tomorrow. That was astonishingly quick by the way. So, thank you in advance for refinishing it for me."

"My pleasure. I like working with wood."

"How did you discover this passion? I can't quite make the correlation from computers to refinishing furniture."

"When I was in college, I already knew I wanted to work for myself, so instead of looking for internships to pad my resume, I looked for jobs that were interesting, paid decently to support myself, and wouldn't interfere with school. I found a carpenter looking for help and all I had to do was be willing to learn. He had a lengthy clientele list; therefore, more work than he and his adult sons could handle. I was one of four kids he hired, and he showed us everything he knew how to do which was impressive. It was a fun job and has become a hobby for me now."

"Did you keep in touch with him? What is his name?" I

sip my coffee and hang on every juicy bit of information coming from a normally reserved Asher.

"Evan. His name was Evan. I did keep in touch after Stanford, but he died a few years ago."

"I'm sorry to hear that, but Evan was probably happy you kept up with what he taught you. All that information goes on with you."

Thank you, Evan, wherever you are, for being good to Asher.

Asher looks thoughtful, his eyes scanning the lake beyond me. "I know he is."

On Tuesday morning, I awake to a pounding headache. Maybe I worked too long a day yesterday, maybe too much screen time while I completed hours of research and purchasing.

My poor abused retinas and my poor abused credit card.

Maybe I didn't hydrate enough yesterday; it was a warm day. Maybe I didn't eat enough. Maybe it's just a tension headache. Regardless, I start my day with two Advil and a tall glass of water, skip the workout, feed Bisou, and make a nutritious breakfast of a veggie egg scramble, orange slices, and jasmine green tea. I choose to eat indoors after sneezing a couple times.

Could I be allergic to something growing here? There are different varieties of flowers and plants in bloom that I'm not used to. I add to today's to-do list a trip to the drugstore for allergy medicine.

I stop by the coffeehouse drive-through across the river for a morning pick me up before Bisou and I meet with a candle artisan about custom creations to sell in the bookstore. We select vessels, scents, label styles, and titles. After hours of essential oils up the nostrils, I'm sneezing up a storm by the time I leave. I've used all of my tissues when I pull into the parking space in front of my future bookstore. Fortunately, my nose has calmed down when I meet with James.

The vintage oak bar is massive and gorgeous with its floral carvings, and in better shape than I thought it would be considering it's from the late 1800s. I can't imagine how heavy it was to lift.

"Oh, the guys brought it in piece by piece and assembled it as you see it now." James laughs.

I guess I wondered that out loud.

"Asher was here when the bar was delivered and said he'll start sanding it down and make any repairs tonight," she states. "We located a cashier counter that is a close match. That will be delivered on Monday."

I look around the spacious room. It's only been days and I already see what the retail space is shaping into. James said the new electrical requests have been completed, and we're just waiting for the chandeliers to be delivered. The new ceiling has been installed, and I see where the wiring pokes through waiting for the lighting fixtures. The smell of drying paint lingers. The wood floors gleam.

"Wow! Your team are miracle workers. I am in awe!"

"Dangle a good amount of overtime and miracles do happen." James winks.

"Overtime? Is that usual for a job like this?"

"No, but Ryan and Asher are eager to get your business open, especially Asher. Asher asked for the bones of this job to be completed as quick as possible without losing quality. As soon as we receive the supplies, we'll begin building the shelving units. As long as we keep receiving our supplies as scheduled, our work should be done during the first week of June."

Asher! My own personal guardian angel.

"My target opening date just became a reality. Thank you for the excellent news."

"You're welcome, but your thanks should be steered toward Asher. We're just doing our jobs as directed by him. Not like he overworks us-he's a great boss. Really fantastic! Everyone loves him!"

Hmmm . . .

This is the second time James has gushed over Asher, and I can't help wondering if she wants him, harbors a crush, or maybe they dated. Or . . . or . . . or. I have to know if I'm stepping on toes. I'm not the kind of woman who fights over a man.

"Sounds like you think highly of Asher."

Yes, I lay it out just like that.

James cocks her head and her faces scrunches, then springs back to life, eyes and mouth widening. "Oh my God! You think I have a thing for Asher?"

Her answer is almost a laugh, and I feel my body relax.

She continues, her expression turning more earnest. "Don't get me wrong, Asher is brilliant and handsome and the nicest guy ever, but can I tell you something?"

I take a step closer. "Of course."

She wrings her hands together, and I wonder if she's changing her mind until her mouth starts forming words. "My interest is with someone else, and until I get over that, I'm useless for anyone else."

James is careful with her wording, leaving the who vague, so I can't guess. Yet I'm me, and I can guess that I've probably met this person, or she thinks I know this person.

"I understand, James. I'm the same way."

"Whew! I think I needed to get that off my chest. I feel so much better. Nothing like talking to a stranger about matters of the heart. You know, Gen-I'm sorry, can I call you Gen?"

"Of course." I think I could be friends with this woman.

"Okay, Gen, you seem like good people, so I confess that the only reason I said all those good things about Asher is, not that all those things aren't true, but I saw the way he couldn't take his eyes off you, and I thought he could use the boost."

"Oh!" I don't blush a lot, but I can feel my cheeks heat to crimson.

"I'm sorry, was that too much information?" James looks so worried that she overstepped.

"No, it's fine. I just didn't expect you to say that."

"I was trying to be a good wingwoman because Asher is so great that I want him to get what he wants in life. I've worked with him for a while, and I've never seen him date and if you have his full attention, well, I don't think Asher would pick someone bad. Shit! I'm babbling!" James covers her face with both her hands.

I wonder what James' story is. I wonder how she became a contractor. I wonder who in her life she has to talk to. I wonder who she has her heart set on that is not returning her affection.

"James . . ." I wait until she lowers her hands before finishing my sentence. "It's okay. I won't repeat what you said."

She looks so relieved. "I better get back to work before my mouth gets me in more trouble."

"Of course, and thanks again. Once this place opens, your coffee will be forever on the house."

"Thanks!" She begins to take backward steps. "I'll keep in touch as things progress."

I wave goodbye and don't stick around because Bisou is snoozing in her carrier after giving up on whining to get out and explore-a definite no with all the danger she can find in a construction area. It's a good thing I step outside when I do, because I receive a text from my mother asking if I'm free for a phone call. Instead of texting back right away, I get Bisou settled in my car, then settle myself in the driver's seat before dialing Maman.

She picks up on the first ring. "Bonjour, ma chérie."

"Bonsoir, Maman." I say no more, deciding to wait and see how she directs the talk I'm about to receive.

"Ça va?"

I hear those two words as I lean my head against the headrest and stare out the windshield, but nothing I see registers in my mind.

"I'm fine. Busy with bookstore projects, but I'm sure that's not of interest to you." I'm well aware that was a bratty thing to say. "Ça va?"

It's quiet on my mother's end until I hear a deep sigh.

"Tu te trompes. I am interested in what interests my children."

"Are you?" This is not me being a brat. I genuinely want to know. "You have never asked me about my business plan."

"Genevieve, I said 'this is not like you' because you have never kept anything this important from me, not because I have a problem with your bookstore."

"My brothers have a problem with my new career."

"I have spoken to them already and told them to let it go."

I have my doubts about Elias, but I will give Maman the benefit of the doubt.

"Simone de Beauvoir is quoted to have once said 'J'accepte la grande aventure d'être moi.' Do you understand what that means?"

"Something about accepting a great adventure?" I look

over my shoulder to check on Bisou, but she's still sound asleep.

"I accept the great adventure of being me," she translates.

I allow the French and English words to sink in. It's a good quote.

Maman continues, "Genevieve, live your life. Oui, Papá and I wanted you and your brothers to work hard and live a good and stable life, but that in no way means at the sacrifice of your happiness. Si tu étais mécontente de ton travail-"

"It wasn't just being unhappy with my job." I need her to understand me because I can't have this conversation again. "I was stuck in everything. And in a city of nearly four million people, I was lonely."

There's the admission I have been keeping to myself because I honestly don't want anyone feeling guilty for accepting the adventure of being them. And why I dated mediocre men.

Maman is quiet again. "I shouldn't have left you."

"Maman, I truly understand why you couldn't stay in LA. My loneliness is not your fault. I needed a fresh start and I have found that here in Buffalo. I have a new purpose, one that makes me excited about work. I'm meeting people. I'm not lonely anymore. And I have the cutest puppy ever."

"Send me pictures."

I know Maman means send her pictures of everything new in my life.

"I will. As soon as I get home."

The weight has lifted from my shoulders. I was lucky to be dealt two good parents. Papá may be gone, but I still have a loving mother. And when I consider someone like Asher who had none, has no one, I embrace all that I have.

"Parle-moi de tom ami. Asher?" She knows very well his name is Asher.

"Asher Adams is my neighbor. We have become fast friends and . . ." I take a deep breath. "I think he has become important to me."

"Je sais." She's smiling the widest, I can tell. "I hear it in your voice."

I hear it too.

Asher

He has never taken care of anyone in his life. It's only been Asher navigating the challenges of getting through childhood and into a responsible adulthood, armed with the few lessons his grandmother taught him during the short time they had together.

One day, Jin steps into his lap, and now, this puppy is quickly rewiring his brain, expanding his capacity to care. Asher is quick to realize, taking care of someone who is important to you is . . . a privilege.

His neighbor, his friend, has quickly become important to Asher, rewiring his brain . . .

His heart . . .

Chapter Seventeen

GENEVIEVE

I t always begins with a little scratch in my throat. A sensation that feels like I need to down a tall glass of water–annoying, yet easy to ignore. Less than a day later, it's a scorching sore throat and it's obvious to me that illness is barreling down like a freight train. Ears, nose, and throat on fire. I don't get sick often, but when I do, I'm a wimp.

The first thing I do is place a delivery order for all the ingredients to make a large stockpot of chicken soup, sans noodles-I'm not a noodle girl. In the order, I include Cara Cara oranges, cold medicines, more boxes of tissues than I need, and immunity boosting teas and juice shots. All my weapons for combat.

I'm about to set my alarm for delivery time and get a couple more hours of sleep when there's a knock at my front door. I can't even think through the fever fog who it could be at 7:30 a.m., then . . .

Crap!

It's Wednesday. I'm supposed to go walking with Asher

and our puppies this morning and have breakfast after. All part of the routine we're trying to set the puppies on.

I hear Bisou stir in her crate beside my bed, and it solidifies my need to get up and be responsible. So, I unlatch the crate door as I amble out of blankets, cough out a 'good morning' to Bisou who is more cheerful than I can handle in this moment, and schlep to the front door. When I open the door, it feels heavier than it is, amplifying the aches throughout my body.

Bisou is so happy to see Asher, wiggling her butt and whimpering at his feet. He picks up my furball with his left hand; his right is full with Jin. He allows Bisou to happily squirm in his arm and lick his chin, but his eyes never leave me. And I know what he sees: rumpled sleep tank and shorts, haphazard ponytail, and absolute misery. I can't muster the energy to care.

He, on the other hand, is his usual handsome self: freshly showered, damp hair curled behind his ears, and dressed casually in a lightweight, long sleeve gray tee and matching sweatpants because the May early mornings aren't exactly warm yet.

"I'm sorry. I forgot our plans for this morning. If you give me five minutes, I'll throw on some clothes." I definitely don't sound like myself.

"What's wrong?" His brows furrow, eyes behind glasses looking me over from mussed hair down my body to my candy apple red painted toes.

"I have a cold." I cough into my elbow.

"What do you need? Can I pick anything up for you? Medicine? Soup?"

"I already scheduled a delivery for everything I need. When it arrives, I'll make soup."

Finally, he looks down at Bisou, and she beams under his attention.

My smitten kitten, I don't blame you.

"I'll take Bisou for a walk. You need to go back to bed."

I can't even argue that Bisou is my baby to take care of when I feel nothing but relief. Instead, I let Asher inside before fetching Bisou's harness and leash from the coat closet.

"Genevieve, please go back to bed. I know where everything is." He takes a few steps into my apartment and finds what he needs in the closet.

"Okay."

Bisou has calmed and is resting comfortably in Asher's arm with her sister. I give her a scratch behind her ear, then say to her, "Be good for Asher."

She gives me a little wag of her tail in answer, whatever that answer may be.

I look up to Asher's face. "Thank you."

He nods. "What time is your delivery supposed to be here?"

"Between nine and ten."

"I want you to rest. I'll be back before then to receive the order and put everything away."

"Who knew you can be bossy?"

His lips twitch. "Only when absolutely necessary."

If my head didn't feel floaty and achy and hot, I might think about Asher being bossy in other ways. Instead, I shuffle over to the small console table near the front door, open the drawer and pull out a tiny plastic baggie.

"I finally got around to having a couple more spare keys made." I open the baggie, fish one out with my fingers, then hand Asher the shiny new silver key.

Asher sets both puppies down on the floor, takes the key from me, and stares at it longer than he should. He looks up. His face may be puzzling, but his tone is sincere.

"Thank you, Genevieve. It means a lot that you trust me in this way."

"Of course I trust you."

Trust and a whole lot more I can't parse out now.

I sneeze into my elbow.

There's that concern on his face again. "Do you need anything before I leave?"

"I'll make myself some tea before I go back to bed."

"I can make tea for you."

"Thank you but just take care of Bisou for now. I'll be fine."

When Asher finishes placing the key I gave him on his own keyring, he bends to place the harness on Bisou, who is barely able to contain her excitement for a walk, then clips the leash on before standing again.

"Text me if you need anything."

I nod, grateful.

Asher guides Bisou and Jin out the front door and casts an unsure glance my way, as if reluctant to leave, before exiting himself.

The sound is distant. Dream-like. If it is a dream, the sound is nice, but the heat in this dream is stifling. Making me sweat, and not in the good, sexy way.

"Wake up for me, Genevieve."

Oh! Asher is the nice sound.

I feel my eyelids resist raising, opening one at a time.

"Asher." I wonder if he heard that because it is barely a sound. My throat is scorching.

"Genevieve, I need you to sit up." His voice is soothing to my ears. "I have medicine here for you to take. Your temperature is high and we need to bring it down."

My brain is cloudy, but I do understand him and nod.

I manage to pull myself upright with Asher's assistance, but I can't call it graceful and I don't really care. He hands me a tiny plastic cup filled with bright orange liquid. I knock it back. He takes the cup from me and hands me a glass of water which I down quickly.

I'm so thirsty.

"You said my temp is high?" I croak out.

Asher unwraps a throat lozenge for me, some sort of berry-looking flavor.

"Yeah. It's hovering at one hundred one."

"No wonder I'm so hot." I take the lozenge and pop it into my mouth. Berry it is. "Did all the soup ingredients arrive?"

"I think so. I put everything in the refrigerator."

I start to get out of bed, but Asher's hands wrap around my shoulders to still me.

"Where are you going?" he asks.

"To make soup."

"You need to stay in bed. I'll make the soup."

"You know how to make soup?" Even raising my eyebrow is an effort.

"No, but you can tell me. I'm not completely useless in the kitchen."

Normally, I'm a control freak in the kitchen, and I could get my butt out of bed to get the soup done. But soup is so easy to assemble, and I really don't want to move.

"Okay." I sigh and think a moment. "The large stockpot is in the cabinet to the right of the stove on the bottom shelf. Place all the chicken thighs and breasts at the bottom of the pot. Peel and quarter both onions. Cut four celery stalks and four carrots in thirds. Crush eight cloves of garlic with the side of the knife blade, then cut them in half."

Asher pulls his cell phone out of his front pocket and quickly thumb types my instructions.

I continue, "Add two bay leaves, four whole cloves, a half teaspoon sage, ten black peppercorns, a teaspoon of pink salt, a half teaspoon red pepper flakes, a half teaspoon ground sage, and a half teaspoon ground ginger. After all the ingredients are in, fill the pot with cold water to about two inches from the rim. Bring the water to a boil over medium high heat. You only need to stir occasionally. Cook the soup for two hours and add water as needed. After it's done cooking, I'll tell you what to do next."

I'm grateful this is not a complicated recipe because my head hurts to think.

"Got it." Asher finishes typing and returns his gaze to me. "Meanwhile, I'd like you to eat something. Perhaps some ice cream for your throat?"

"I don't think I have ice cream in my freezer." My voice sounds so small to me.

Asher smiles. "I brought over that strawberry one you like so much. Unless you want chocolate or orange cream."

I blink a few times, stunned he remembered all my favorites. And I can't help it; I go gooey inside regardless of how bad I feel. "Strawberry sounds good."

Asher stands from the edge of my bed and heads toward my bedroom door. "I'll be right back."

I know I should stay in bed. I know I should leave Asher alone in the kitchen to complete his tasks. But I can't. One slow leg at a time goes over the edge of the bed and when both feet are on solid ground, I ease myself up. I grab my box of tissues and head out to the kitchen.

Asher immediately notices me, stopping mid-scoop of ice cream to assess me, eying me up and down, probably to make sure I'm not about to fall on my face.

"You trust me with the key to your home, but not with your kitchen." He places the cover back on the ice cream container when he's done.

I sidle up to the counter and take a seat on the stool at the end. "I don't usually eat in bed."

"And you can't make an exception when you're sick?"

"Especially when I'm sick. What if I misjudge my hand to mouth coordination and the ice cream-laden spoon drops to the sheets? Then I have to change the sheets, and that's more of a pain in the butt when sick."

Asher sets the small bowl of two scoops of strawberry pink heaven in front of me with a spoon jutting out. I don't hesitate to dig in and allow the creamy cold goodness to melt on my tongue. I swallow, and my throat feels a thousand times better–ice cream is magic! Or the medicine is kicking in.

He crosses his arms across his chest. "Or you don't trust I can follow your instructions for the soup."

I snort. "Your STEM brain calling a recipe 'instructions.'"

Asher chuckles. "Recipe is just a fancy word for instructions."

I've already devoured one of the scoops of ice cream. I'm hungrier than I thought.

"Asher, thank you for taking care of Bisou and the ice cream, but you've been around me enough today. Honestly, I will feel horrible if you were to get sick. Where is my daughter, by the way?"

Asher stares at me, analyzing me with that big brain of his. I know he sees my discomfort in him taking care of me.

"Bisou and Jin are currently expending copious amounts of puppy energy in the playpen next door. I didn't want their yapping to wake you." He returns the carton of ice cream to the freezer and begins to retrieve the soup ingredients from the refrigerator. "I rarely get sick. So, I'm staying. You'll finish your ice cream and go back to bed or camp out on your sofa. I'll assemble the soup, check on the pups, and bring my laptop over to get some work done. Okay?"

"Okay." A whisper from my mouth again.

Is that submission?

"Good. I'll wake you when the soup is done. Do you want to nap in your bed or on the sofa?"

"Sofa."

While I finish the last gloriously soothing bites of ice cream, Asher makes a cozy bed for me on my sofa using my comforter and pillows from my bed and a set of sheets he found in the linen closet.

I go to rinse my bowl and spoon in the sink, then begin to make myself a mug of tea, but Asher stops me.

"Please go to bed, Genevieve. I'll bring your tea to you when it's done."

"So bossy," I mutter, but I do as I'm told. As I settle in the nest Asher prepared for me, he sets a tall glass of water and a box of tissues on the coffee table. I fall asleep to the rhythmic sound of chopping vegetables.

The combination of puppy whimpers, the delicious perfume of homemade soup, and Asher's soothing tone wakes me. My eyes flutter open and focus on Asher, standing in front of the sofa, hovering over me.

"It's time for more medicine, soup is done, and the kids were missing you." His eyes focus on my face.

I sit up and notice I kicked off the blankets during my nap, probably because I was overheated. Then I realize what

I was too fuzzy brained to see earlier. I'm wearing a matching sleep shorts and tank top set. Thin, soft cotton. No bra. And the shorts are meant for a woman with less ass than I have, so the tiny ensemble leaves, basically, nothing to the imagination. It's comfortable to sleep in, but probably not what Asher bargained for.

I'm suddenly unsure of what to do. Cover myself up again? Or own it because Asher already saw everything? Asher maintains eye contact with me, so, yes, he did see everything. And I feel heated in an entirely different way.

He continues, "I didn't want to wake you, so I looked up a top-rated chicken soup recipe to see what to do next. I strained the broth, shredded the chicken and put it back in the broth with sliced carrots and celery, but left it at that."

He hands me my medicine and a glass of water. I take a couple sips of water before downing the shot of orange liquid and finish the glass of water. He takes the water glass from me and sets it on the table, then picks up both wiggly furballs and places them in my lap. Instant happiness.

"I can't believe I slept through all that."

"You were out cold. You didn't hear me leave or return when I took the pups out before I turned the soup on, nor when I went to my place when the chicken was cooling. I wasn't necessarily quiet either. How do you feel?"

"Not fabulous, but not as horrific as when I woke up this morning."

Asher nods his understanding. "You should have some soup. You haven't eaten much today."

I shift the bundles of puppy joy off my lap before they begin to settle in and let them get cozy together on the sheet-covered cushion. I notice my bare legs again. All that bare skin on display. I have worn denim shorts in front of Asher before, but my sleepwear might as well be underwear.

"Um. Maybe I'll go get my robe first."

Asher leans forward, so close I can feel his space merging with mine. He reaches behind my back for something I can't see until he pulls something pale yellow into view.

My robe.

Asher

After four consecutive days of close proximity to her, this first morning without is an adjustment back to Asher's usual life that he likens to a circus lion tamer with his whip in one hand and chair in the other forcing the lion of all Asher's growing desires back in his cage. He was given a taste of what life could be like, but he's been put back in his box.

Chapter Eighteen

GENEVIEVE

I was down for four days.

For four solid days, Asher took care of me like no man ever had before. Not only did he make the soup, take care of Bisou, and make sure I was taking medicine on time and staying hydrated, each day he went to my bookstore and took video of the progress. He bought me eucalyptus shower bombs and an essential oil diffuser. He kept my apartment clutter-free and threw out my garbage. When I went to take a shower at the end of day two, he changed my sheets and threw the others in the wash.

I tried to send him home, really I did, but all he said was, "No." It could be the finality of the no, or the stone-like quality of Asher's face that conveyed he will not budge on this. I've had boyfriends before, not that Asher is my boyfriend, but during each relationship I can't tell you of one man who wanted to take care of me like this. Okay, one had hot and sour soup delivered to me from a local Chinese restaurant, but that was the extent of that. Furthermore, said man broke up with me two days later because I was still sick and couldn't be his arm candy for a work event of his.

"If you can't be there for me, why am I even with you," said Dickhead. I was not sad he was gone.

Each day, Asher made me his priority. When he had to leave me, he told me when he would return and stuck to it. Each time he returned home, to my home, he checked on me and assured me he was here. I felt that. Felt it so deep in my heart, I thought I might cry in front of him.

On day four, I moved from bed to sofa for a change in scenery. Asher worked on his laptop at my kitchen counter, and when he had to take a call, he went on my balcony and closed the sliding glass door behind him. When he thought I was napping, I watched him type on the largest laptop I've ever seen; code stuff, I think. Watched him analyze blue-prints, make annotations. Watched his fingers move confi-dently and quickly over the keyboard, his strong shoulders relaxed under the heather blue cotton. This is a person who is at ease with their work and knows exactly what to do. In complete command of who they are.

It's sexy.

And it's that thought right there that jolts me like a lightning bolt ricocheting in my chest cavity. I feel like I'm breaking out in a sweat and it's not from a fever.

I thought Asher was attractive the moment I met him but dismissed it because he looked different from the men I've dated in the last ten years. I ignorantly thought that these men were who I should be with. These were boyfriend imposters, and I fell for it because they wore suits and were men that had the types of 'good' jobs parents go gooey for. They spent a decent amount of time with me, but they never cared to know me–they thought the breadcrumbs they doled out were good enough and, foolish me, I accepted it.

Fourteen feet away from me is a man who had no one to teach him how to be a good man, but he figured it out. He had no one to teach him how to take care of someone, but he figured it out. Because of his heart of platinum, he figures shit out.

How could I not love and be in love with Asher?

Yes, I love Asher Adams and it is the truest feeling ever my heart has felt.

This morning, physically, I feel one hundred percent better. Emotionally? I can't even begin to assess.

As I throw on a coral-colored maxi dress, gold hoop earrings and bracelets, and high-heeled espadrilles, I don't know what I'm dressing for. November did invite me to Sunday brunch if I felt better, but I'm not sure I'm in the mood for socializing. Not when I'm feeling . . . unsettled.

When my curls are sufficiently tamed, I place both my hands on the bathroom counter and stare at my reflection, bracing myself for what I know in my gut feels right. And I'm terrified.

I head into the living room, plop Bisou into her carrier, grab my keys, then head out. Once outside my front door, I stand still, sensing anything out of sorts with what I'm about to do, but I find nothing other than my galloping heart. I turn to my right, take three steps, and knock on Asher's door.

When Asher answers, his face brightens. "I wasn't expecting-" Asher's smile falters when he sees my dress. "Wait! Did we have plans I forgot?"

I smile because, of course, he would begin to panic over such a thing.

"No, we don't. Are you busy? Do you have a few minutes to spare?"

He grins again. "Of course."

Asher steps aside to let me inside his apartment. I exhale as I step inside, inhale as I pass Asher, catching the scent of his warm, clean cotton T-shirt and santal soap. Bisou wants out of her carrier, but we won't be here long. I swear my heart is bouncing around my ribcage wanting out too. Not to escape, but I swear, to be closer to the object of its desire.

I can't bear to take another step. I turn in not even the middle of the hallway to face Asher, who abruptly halts as to not crash into me. He looks genuinely surprised, then his eyes narrow, searching my face; an expression I've become very familiar with while I was sick. I am the focal point of his attention; not even an eager-to-be-pet Bisou nor Jin prancing about our legs can distract him.

"Asher, I think . . . No, I don't think." I shake my head, then stop to peer into his intensely beautiful, questioning eyes. Nothing is in focus but him. "I know. I'm falling in love with you."

Asher leans back against the wall, or maybe the world tilts. He folds his arms across his chest and looks at me for a long time. Time stands still.

"How do you know that's how you feel?" His voice is indescribable, not any one thing I can interpret.

I look back at him, deep into his eyes, and realize he's being genuine, not evasive of his feelings. "I just do."

Asher continues to watch my face without blinking. Says nothing. And the moment stretches beyond what is acceptable to wait for any response.

"Okay." I clear my throat and take one slow step backward after another toward the front door. "I just want you to know what I've been thinking and feeling lately."

Just as I begin to turn around to leave, Asher catches my wrist in his hand, a light touch against my skin, halting my motion. I raise my eyes to his, but he doesn't move, doesn't look at me. Instead, he lets go.

Without looking back, I know Asher hasn't moved as I shut the door behind me.

Asher

Asher stands there, back against the hallway wall, unmoving. Stunned. It isn't until Jin, sitting in the middle of the hall, floppy black ears straining to listen, saucer eyes trained on the front door, hoping her sister comes back to play, cries, that Asher snaps out of his trance. He bends down to scoop up his distressed puppy into his arms to comfort her.

"I know. I'm sorry," Asher whispers to Jin, and maybe to himself. "I'm not built for this. I'm sorry."

Chapter Nineteen

A s soon as November sees me, her smile turns into an instant frown. "What's wrong? Your outfit is too beautiful for that face you're making."

I drove around for a while, trying to decide what to do with myself. No way was I going home to sit in my apartment, a wall away from the man I told I love not even an hour ago. Instead, I made the safer decision to lose myself in the Morgan-Day Family Sunday Brunch. Even though I'm feeling extra tender about not having family of my own here to soften the blow of this morning, it's a comfort to have a sister in November and a standing brunch invite.

"I told Asher."

It's all I have to say for November to know what I mean and hug me.

"And he didn't say it back?" she whispers so no one else can hear, yet I see Rhys eying his bride-to-be. His brow furrows, wondering what is fretting his love and how he can fix it.

I've said it once, I'll say it again and again—*I love Rhys for November!*

I whisper back, "He didn't say anything at all."

She releases me from our hug to look me in my eyes. "He will. I'm positive. There's no way he just nursed you back to health for four days and doesn't love you. This is Asher. I may not know him as well as you do, but I know he has some issues I don't know the extent of. I also know he's a good person, and he will come through for you."

I look back into the warm eyes of my gorgeous friend, her hair pulled up in a high, thick braid, a little berry lip gloss on those perfectly shaped lips of hers, and she's wearing a magenta halter summer dress.

"You look beautiful too, by the way," I state.

Rhys steps up, wraps an arm around November's waist and plants a kiss to the crown on her head. "She truly is."

November looks up to him, and I can almost see the unspoken conversation they're having. Rhys asking if everything is alright. November telling him that it's girl stuff that he doesn't need to concern himself with. Him saying if she needs anything, then her cutting him off by saying, *I'll let you know*. Their gazes linger, exuding all the love they have for each other.

Exactly what I want for myself.

Fortunately for me, Gareth is missing from brunch; he's away for the weekend in NYC. I don't think I could handle being prodded by him about Asher right now. Fortunately for me, everyone at the table is the distraction I need. The activity, especially November's sweet niece, Plum, being completely enamored of Bisou, is a start. The conversation, too, particularly Plum hinting for a dog to her parents, works at pushing the thoughts of Asher to the back of my brain. My mind never completely lets him go. How could it?

When I'm back in my SUV, driving the long way home, Asher comes back to the front. I don't regret confessing my feelings. Regardless of the outcome, I need to know how I will be dealing with this love I'm feeling. Will I be allowed to unleash it? Or will I have to box it up? If Asher isn't ready for that conversation, I can be patient, but telling my truth was important.

Bisou has fallen asleep in her carrier, and I'm grateful. I'm tired myself; big emotions will do that to you. I could use a nap and I'm not a nap person. I park the car, Bisou's usual sign to at least pick her head up to determine whether it's worth it to stay awake, but she doesn't stir. She's out cold even as I shut my door and open hers to retrieve her. She shifts a little as I enter the elevator yet remains zonked out.

When I turn the corner into the vestibule Asher and I share, I find him sitting on the ground with his back against my door, arms resting on bent knees, curved into himself, looking thoughtful and sad. He doesn't look up, just stares at his hands resting on his knees. The closer I get, I see the tiny, napping Jin sprawled across his lap.

I set Bisou's carrier on the floor and smooth the skirt of my dress under me before taking a seat beside Asher, legs extended in front of me. There's a significant silence between us before he begins in a low, haggard voice.

"I missed you."

My heart feels like a paperweight in my chest, heavy and pinning me down. Asher must hear me inhale to speak, because he raises his hand in a listless halting sign.

Still looking at his hands, he continues, "While missing you, all I could do was turn your words of falling in love over and over again. I thought about that, and I realized it felt good to have that knowledge." He blows out a breath. "Then I got scared because I thought if you knew what you were feeling for me is love, then you know what love feels like because you're experienced it before."

"I . . . have." At the time I felt those strong feelings for someone, I believed I felt love, but I know what I feel for Asher is so much more powerful. I don't say this because I'm not here to plead a case. I won't try to convince him to love me back, even though I want to scream, *LOVE ME!!!*

Asher nods slightly. "But that love ended."

"It did. Sometimes it doesn't work out. Sometimes it isn't as right as you originally thought."

He nods again, his voice a near whisper as if speaking to himself. "That's what I thought." Finally, his sad, lost gaze meets my hopeful one. "What if it ends with me?"

I don't know what to say. I love fictional happy endings, but in reality, lasting love is not guaranteed. All I can do is muster as much love into my eyes and project it, and hope Asher can see it, feel it. But his eyes return to his hands, and mine sting while focusing on the floral embroidery at the hem of my dress covering my ankles.

He continues, "I haven't had anyone love me for decades. Never romantic love. When I'm with you, I feel your care; I forgot what that feels like. Now that I have it, I don't want to lose it, but I don't know how to be like you."

"I don't want you to be like me." I turn my head to look at him, to search for any sign of where this is leading. "I love you for who you are."

"I've never had this." Finally, he looks to me. "I'm afraid, Genevieve. I've never had this." His inhale is shaky before he continues. "You're, you. Blindingly, brilliant you. The brightest sun to my dull world. I don't think I could survive you choosing to leave me when you decide I'm not enough. I'm never enough for anyone. I'm afraid I'm going to become too clingy, and you'll loathe me for it. I'll be too much, and you won't love me anymore."

Carefully, I pick up Jin from Asher's lap, then set her in Bisou's carrier. They smush together and instantly fall back to sleep. I climb into his lap, the best my dress will allow. I need him to feel me, my solid presence, warm body to warm body. This startles him. Good. I want him to understand I won't let him go.

His shimmery eyes are impossibly bright behind his glasses as he holds my tear-filled gaze.

"Asher, I need you to not only hear my words, I need you to allow them seep into your skin, your veins, your heart." Tears tumble over my bottom lashes. "I want to be overwhelmed by your love. I've never had that before and it is so much of what I've desired from life. There is no such thing as too much love for someone who wants it. Overwhelm me, Asher Adams. I dare you to bowl me over with your love."

Asher reaches for my hands, gently lacing his fingers with mine. He brings them to his lips and kisses the top of one hand, then the other.

"I'm not falling in love with you, Genevieve." He places both my hands to the space on his chest over his heart, then covers them with his own. "I already love you. And I'll do anything to keep you, because I don't want to go back to a life without the sun."

"I love you, Asher." My voice is watery; my heart is bursting.

He loves me!

Asher reaches up to cup my jaw to wipe away the tears with soothing swipes of his thumbs, then one of those thumbs traces the line of my cheekbone down to my plush bottom lip. I can't tell if Asher is trembling or if it's me. His eyes dip down to my lips.

"May I kiss you, Genevieve?" Asher's voice is a quiver as his hopeful eyes meet mine.

I've never been asked to be kissed before, and that's another of the numerous ways in which Asher shows he cares: consent.

"Yes, you may," I answer, another tear escaping its eyelash boundary.

He leans forward and gently presses his soft lips to the tear and kisses it away; my eyes flutter closed. I feel his warm breath on my cheek as he trails light kisses down my jawline, and I shiver. He wraps one arm around my waist, simultaneously pulling me closer and holding me still. My eyes open when I feel his thumb smooth across my bottom lip.

"Your lips are so lovely," he whispers. "So unbelievably tempting."

I can feel the compliment land on my skin, and I swear, if it could, my skin would glow as if I was really his sun.

His thumb moves aside, and Asher moves closer, his face a blur as his lips first touch mine. Featherlight. A brush stroke. A firmer slide as my eyelids lower, and Asher is kissing me like I have never been kissed before: a communication of how deeply he adores me. His hand is lost in my hair, his arm tight around me. I plant my hands on his firm chest and grip his T-shirt as his tongue asks for permission to explore my mouth. My lips part for him and he takes the kiss deeper. Tongues tasting, caressing each other. I feel his passion for me through his jeans and I revel in it. I want more. I want to see naked Asher unhinged.

A low moan escapes my throat, and Asher's response is to slow the kiss down until a natural break. Although my mouth laments not being attached to Asher's anymore, my mind knows it's a wise decision to stop since we are where any neighbor on our floor could walk by and see us.

"Do you want to come inside?" I ask with a raspy voice.

Asher cups the back of my neck, looking deep into my eyes as if to make sure I hear him.

"I do, but I won't. Because if I do, I'm going to want . . . everything."

"What's wrong with everything? I want everything with you."

"Nothing at all." His smile shines like I have never seen, and I want to bask in it. "But I want this moment right now. We told each other, 'I love you.' We shared our first kiss. I want to savor this. I want to do this right and take you out on a date."

I think a moment. I think how we have been spending time together, and it has been way more fun than a stuffy date.

"We don't need to date. I love the way we are together. It's been fun getting to know each other the way we have. Why do we need to date?"

Asher watches the back of his fingers stroke my cheek, and there is wonder in his eyes, maybe wonder that he gets to touch me the way he is.

"Our time together has been the best hours of my life."

I hear those words. I equally love and hate that they are true.

He continues, "I still would like to take you out tomorrow, if you're free. You don't have to look at it as a date, just spending the day together."

"I am free and would love to spend the day with you."

He kissed me first, but I want to know that this will never be one way. He needs to know I don't only love him; I *want* him. I lean forward, wrap my arms around his neck, and kiss him on the lips.

Keeping it PG . . . this time.

Asher

"*Our first date!*" *Asher grins to himself as he packs up the supplies he needs for today's outing. He never allowed himself to imagine going out on a date with her, so he spent the remainder of Sunday planning and shopping and preparing, all the while opening the door to wishing just a crack, maybe a little more.*

She is everything he could imagine and never dared to wish for.

Chapter Twenty

GENEVIEVE

All Asher said was for me to dress casually for a warm, sunny Memorial Day on the water. I took that to mean we would most likely be taking the kayaks out on the lake, so I slather myself in sunscreen before pulling my curls into a high braid and swiping Piña Colada Lip Smacker on my lips, then dress in my hibiscus print white bikini, cutoff denim shorts, and old sneakers. I pack a book-turned-beach tote (what I do with all my book totes that have seen better days) with a pair of sandals, my pink dad hat embroidered with Book Babe (a past birthday gift from November), a lightweight hoodie (just in case), beach towel, skincare essentials, and my dry bag. Asher told me only Bisou's harness and leash are necessary for this outing; he will supply the rest.

My heart is fluttering all over the place as my mind replays how Asher told me he loves me. Remembering every syllable, every touch of his fingers-THAT KISS! Asher Adams can make my toes curl with a kiss! Now, all I want is to be near him and know it wasn't all a dream.

I invited him over for breakfast this morning, but he

declined, stating he had to "get ready for our non-date" and "if I saw you now, nothing will get done" which made me smile until my face hurt. I will give him this. Okay, I will admit what this is, a date, because Asher wants it so much. I have to remind myself that all this is relatively new to him, where I have had plenty through my life. Yet I know in my gut that this date will be like no other because, simply, it's with Asher.

At ten a.m., Asher is knocking at my front door. His lips part, no, I think his jaw drops when I open the door, as his eyes behind glasses become wider and darker as he takes me in head to toe and back again. Yes, he's seen much more of my skin while I was sick, but now he's seeing me when he has touched me, kissed me, and he obviously likes what he sees very, very much. While Bisou and Jin, both on leash, greet each other, I rise on my tip toes to give Asher a kiss hello and, I swear, I feel his entire body sigh as if he too needed to know this is real.

"Good morning," I say in the most idiotic giddy way.

"Good morning, Love."

'Love' escapes his lips as if longing to come out. Goose bumps break out all over my skin at hearing this new nickname, and from the feeling of his smile against my lips as he kisses me this time.

I make Asher smile!

He takes my tote from my shoulder and carries it all the way to his truck, which looks newly detailed, shinier than usual. We secure the puppies and their supplies in the backseat, then Asher opens the passenger side door for me to climb in. Although I'm getting the hang of the high step-up, he still offers me his hand. But before I sit, I see a bag of Red Vines waiting for me. I pick up the bag, take my seat, but before he can close the door, I grab Asher by the front of his T-shirt, pull him close, and crash my lips against his.

When I release him, Asher looks dazed, his eyes unfocused and his eyeglasses askew. It feels like tiny champagne bubbles swirl through my veins over having this effect on him. I right the glasses on his nose.

"Is that a normal 'thank you' kiss from you?" he gasps.

"It is for you, why?"

"You need to warn a guy," he says before closing my door.

Still feeling light and fizzy, I tear open the bag of Red Vines. When Asher slides into the driver's seat, I say, "I knew we would be taking the kayaks out, but I didn't know we would be driving somewhere."

He turns over the ignition and "Iris" by The Goo Goo Dolls instantly fills the cabin. He proceeds to back out of his parking space. "We can kayak around here anytime. I have a special place I want to show you and, I hope, it will be just you and me."

"I hope so too."

I mean it. I want Asher all to myself. I want all his attention. I want to kiss him without prying eyes. I want to have uninterrupted conversation. I want to be alone in a classroom and learn all about him.

I hold out a short rope of red licorice for Asher to take.

He leans forward and takes the licorice with his teeth, then threads his fingers through mine, holding my hand on the console between us, and we are on our way.

We drive for about an hour outside the city; I haven't a clue where I am, and I don't ask because I'm leaning into the surprise. We pass lush green landscapes and flashes of lake views before Asher slows to turn onto a narrow grass and dirt clearing flanked by nondescript bushes and trees. Not exactly a road, but a strip of land that has been driven on over time.

"Isn't this private property?" I ask. "I saw some homes along the way."

"This little slice is public." Asher drives slowly and I know it's to not jostle us. Not jostle me. "One day, I was looking for somewhere new to kayak and pulled up some detailed maps on my computer."

Just as he finishes his sentence, the vegetation gives way to a picturesque view of Lake Erie. He gently applies the brakes to allow me my initial look.

He continues, "I discovered this tiny, seemingly untouched, beach with calm water. I thought it would be a good spot to test the puppies on the kayaks."

"What?" That turns my head. "How?"

Asher begins a three-point turn in the tight space. "I bought them life jackets and outfitted our kayaks with some dog comfort features. We'll only take them out for a little while to see how they adapt to being out on the water."

"I barely know how to take care of myself on a kayak."

He positions the truck so we're facing the way we came, sets the truck in park, then turns off the ignition. "That's why I'll take Jin and Bisou on my kayak. When you get your bearings, we'll put Bisou on yours for a while."

"Okay. I think I can do that."

"I know you can."

I take care of the puppies, allow them to test their footing on the sand/pebble combo of this tiny crescent beach, and they respond in an ear perked up, slow movement, noses sniffing overtime, pawing the ground sort of way that makes me laugh. Asher laughs at the scene as he places the second kayak down near the water's edge.

Asher . . . laughed!

It isn't a burst out loud laugh like mine; it's a laugh almost like he's testing it out because it hasn't appeared in a long time, a low sound that comes from the chest rather than the belly. Yet it's real and happy and I could cry. I chomp down on a piece of licorice instead.

The puppies last forty minutes on the kayaks before we can tell they are completely wiped out from sensory overload. Bisou spends the last ten minutes on my kayak, trying to get comfortable in my lap, and it feels like I'm holding my breath the entire time. Jin misses her sister and attempts to walk on water but her dad hauls her back. Frustrated, she gnaws at his hand which Asher has to scold her for, which takes a toll on him having to reprimand his baby girl. I have to look away, so he won't see me bite my lips to contain a laugh. Asher's heart is so soft, and I wouldn't have it any other way.

I float near the shore while Asher pulls his kayak on land. I watch how he takes care of Jin, settles her on a towel, and how she looks at him like he is the center of her universe. I think about how he has taken care of me with not only my business needs, but when I was sick or when he went to Canada to get me Chinese food because he wanted me to have the best. The water socks currently on my feet. I think about this purple kayak I'm currently sitting on, and I don't need anyone to tell me that he bought this special for me. I won't mention it because it will only embarrass him.

My move to Buffalo feels right in every way. Meant to be.

After Asher assists Bisou and me off my kayak and returns the equipment to the truck bed, we work together to set out the picnic lunch he packed on a thick camping blanket. Asher sets out two bowls of puppy food, which Bisou and Jin wolf down, then heap together in a shady part of the blanket and fall fast asleep.

We eat a well-planned, healthy lunch of grilled vegetable and smoked mozzarella wrap sandwiches, a very colorful fruit salad, and unsweetened iced jasmine green tea. All deliciously homemade by Asher's hands, and I have mad respect for him making food for me when he could have easily purchased it from a restaurant.

When we are almost done with lunch, we receive a text at the same time. I look first because the only person who might text us is November, and I'm curious what she could possibly need from both of us, but it's James. She sent pictures of the cashier counter that was delivered this morning. I lean into Asher to show him the images on my cell phone screen. It feels so good to be close to him like this.

"It's gorgeous," Asher states. "I can't wait to get my hands on it."

I can't wait until he gets his hands on me.

I clear my throat. "It is."

"I'm nearly done with the bar. When are you scheduling equipment delivery?"

"I have employee interviews on Wednesday; equipment delivery on Friday. As soon as I have my baristas, I can schedule training with the espresso machine company. I'll go through the training as well."

"Just in case." He plops the final bite of his sandwich into his mouth and chews.

"Just in case," I repeat. I remember what I have been meaning to tell Asher. "Thank you for being on my side, for believing in my business."

Asher looks embarrassed but doesn't hesitate to set the record straight. "I hope you know I didn't help you because I'm romantically interested in you. I truly believe the coffee bar alone will be a benefit to the tenants in the building and the surrounding community, but I also believe the bookstore will pull in customers from near and far. I did the research. I'd be an idiot not to have your business in my building." He grins and takes my hand that rests on the blanket beside him in his. "I will admit that I like the idea of having you close by. I would like to park myself at a table in the corner with my laptop and work while being able to look up and see you. Maybe you take a break to have coffee with me, and we catch up with each other for a moment."

He paints a vivid picture for my brain, and it sees what he's imagining for us. My bookstore fully alive. Maybe I'm creating a table display of autumn romances, placing the finishing touches just after opening and Asher is one of the first in the coffee order line. When I'm done, I join him at the pick-up counter and give him a kiss hello. We take our coffees to a lone bistro table with two chairs by the window that is reserved just for him to work and for me to join him when I can. A future that is only a few weeks away.

My smile cannot be contained. "I am in love with that idea, very much."

For several heartbeats, Asher's gaze holds mine, then he shifts his body to the right for a better angle to cup my face in both his hands, stroking the warm skin of my cheeks with his thumbs, my body leaning toward him like a flower following the sun.

His Adam's apple bobs. "I am in love with you, so very much."

He doesn't wait for a response. His lips crash against mine like it's the only thing they have wanted to do since we last kissed. We are so in sync when our lips part and our tongues find each other to touch, to taste, to explore. Asher reaches across me, his hand grips my bare waist, the right claiming pressure, and I feel it zing me to my core. I bury my fingers into his hair and pull him closer. Asher whimpers, his kiss turning frenzied, and he nearly lowers me to the blanket. But we part when we hear a speedboat blaze by, close enough to feel aware we are in public and the lake is littered with boats and jet skis on this fine holiday afternoon.

Asher's forehead rests against mine while he catches his breath, each of his hands holding one of mine. He brings the right to his lips for a brush of his lips, then the left, leaving a kiss on my ring finger.

"Genevieve, will you be my girlfriend?"

"Since we've told each other 'I love you,' I kind of thought I already was."

He pulls back enough to look me in the eyes; his hazel is impossibly warm.

"I want my intentions to be ultra-clear. I want you to always know where you stand with me."

There's something about the seriousness of his words that soothes something inside me. Security. Stability. Safety. Care. Love. That's the man Asher is. Perhaps someday I'll discover how he learned to be such a good man, because I do want to know; no, I will know.

"Yes, Asher, I am yours." I reach up to cup his cheek and he leans into my touch, soaking up my affection like a sponge. "And you are mine."

Security. Stability. Safety. Care. Love.

All on offer, all taken.

Asher

Before, Asher didn't fully understand what he was missing. He has meaningful work that challenges him and an abundance of hobbies and interests to fill his time. He has a home and money to help him feel secure, never having to worry about the basic necessities of life the way he so often did as a kid and through college.

Now, Asher understands that his life was missing one truly important component, one that far outweighs the others, and her name is Genevieve Torres.

Chapter Twenty-One

GENEVIEVE

When we return to our apartment building, the afternoon is still young, and more people than I have seen around the river are taking advantage of a gorgeous day off from work. I hear competing music in the distance coming from boats sailing by and the restaurants that sound so much closer than they actually are. It's one big party.

I take our groggy doggies on a short walk to relieve themselves while Asher cleans off the kayaks and unpacks his truck. Together, Asher and I ride the elevator up to our floor, puppies looking like they might fall asleep standing up. I have my beach bag on my shoulder, and Asher carries everything else.

When we step off the elevator, I remember when I first saw Asher, sitting on the floor, reading pages from a romance novel. It feels so long ago, definitely not just a month. Who knew that stranger would become so significantly important to me? Who knew that stranger would become the man I fell hard for?

Asher walks slightly ahead, and I know he wants to reach my door to open it for me. I watch the movement of his shoulders, his back through his T-shirt. When he halts in our vestibule, I see his head move slightly from his door to my door, and I understand he isn't sure which to open first.

"Let's go to your apartment." I decide for us. "You're carrying more stuff than I am."

"Do you want to drop your bag off first?" he asks.

"Nope."

He selects a key from his ring and unlocks his door, holding it open for me to pass through with the puppies. I kick off my sandals and hear the click of the lock shutting behind us as I continue down the hallway to the puppy pen in the living room, then unharness the dogs and place them inside where they immediately cozy up to each other and drift off to what looks to be a long rest after a handful of adventurous hours.

Asher has already begun to unpack anything that needs to be cleaned, placing dog bowls and picnic dishes into the sink to be rinsed, the clinks against stainless steel the only sound in his spacious apartment. The closer I get to Asher, the thicker the tension becomes. If I can feel it, I'm positive he can too.

Before he can grab another thing from a bag, I place my hand on his and feel him tremble. I lace my fingers with his and guide him across the open plan areas to his bedroom, pass the neatly made king-sized bed, and step into the large bathroom with a separate shower and bathtub.

When I turn to face Asher, his eyes look rounder, darker, unmoving from me. I reach behind my neck and untie the top of my bikini, then quickly the back and allow the top to drop to the floor. Asher sucks in his breath, but he doesn't look down, his eyes trained on mine. I unwind the hair tie at the bottom of my braid, toss it to the counter, then unravel the braid to the top tie and toss that too. My hair is soft and wavy down my back. Next, I unbutton and unzip my shorts, pushing them down, taking my bikini bottoms with them to the tiled floor, never taking my eyes off Asher's.

I relish the feeling of being completely naked while Asher is fully clothed with the exception of his rather nice-looking feet. I step closer, allow my eyes to wander downward as I take the edge of his T-shirt in my fingers. My eyes dart up, raising an eyebrow in question. Asher knows what I'm asking as he nods. I pull his T-shirt upward; my knuckles graze against the firm plains of his abdomen, his chest. He flinches from my touch, but I know it's not in a bad way. Who knows how long it's been since he's been touched like this?

He doesn't touch me without my permission, which I haven't given yet, but he does slowly raise his arms to tug his shirt over his head; I can't reach that high. After a quick straightening of his eyeglasses, his eyes glance at the T-shirt on top of my discarded clothing, then focuses on my feet for long seconds, mustering the courage, with a deep inhale, to look at all my naked skin. He slowly casts a glance to my strong, smooth legs, trailing upward to the apex of my thighs, where his eyes linger, and he licks his lips.

The thrill of what I'm doing to him ricochets through my body.

His stare becomes bolder, more eager, as his eyes move over the hourglass of my shape, to my full breasts, their pinkish brown nipples, then skim my neck to return to my face.

"You devastate me, Genevieve. Beautiful is not strong enough of a word." He exhales. "How did I deserve-"

"Shhhhh . . ." I cut him off. "There is no question of what you deserve."

I step a little closer. My fingers toy with the drawstring of his board shorts. "May I?"

"Please," he quickly answers, making me smile wide as I gently tug the knot until undone.

The bulge in his shorts is undeniable-he's so hard it has to hurt. Asher's breath quickens at the sound of Velcro ripping apart. My fingers skim along the underside of his veined cock as I set him free of his shorts. Long and thick, his cock stands at attention, and it strikes me for a second how that will fit inside me, but we'll cross that bridge. All I know for sure is I will be soaking wet ready to try.

"I'm nervous." His voice is choked. "It's been an extremely long time." He swallows, hard. "And the few times I have . . ." His eyes shut, reopen. "I want this more. I want you so much more."

"You may not understand it . . ," I keep my voice clear as a bell. "But I want you so much more too, Asher."

He nods. "Condoms. I bought condoms."

I smirk at my thoughtful planner of a boyfriend.

Boyfriend. I'm his and he is mine.

"Good to know. I'm on birth control, but we'll definitely be using condoms too."

I take his hand in mine and lead him to the shower. He opens the glass door, reaches inside to turn the knob, testing the temperature of the water spray with his fingers before allowing me entry. He removes his eyeglasses, sets them on the bathtub ledge, then steps in behind me. The enclosed shower space is not small, but even with his lean muscle mass, Asher's height and width of his shoulders takes up space.

There was no plan behind getting Asher to shower with

me. I'm going on instinct here. I knew being naked with a woman wasn't a recent memory for him. As much as I am dying to see him come apart and to come apart in return, I want to ease his nerves more.

First, I take good look at his body, streams of water caressing defined muscle, smooth skin, a happy trail slightly darker than the hair on his head, and a cloud-shaped birthmark at the top of his right thigh. My head automatically nods approval; I really like what I see. Yet, I also know in my heart, forty years from now, I'll still like what I see. Simply because it's Asher.

I tilt my head back and look Asher in his eyes and give him the words he gave to me. "Beautiful is not strong enough a word."

Asher's eyes shut, his eyebrows furrow, his lips turn into a grimace-my words don't easily penetrate what remains of his shield. If I stepped inside his head, his memories, I'm positive I would not find words of adoration given to him.

Let me be the one to give him words of love over and over then.

I reach for the bar of soap on the ledge, wet it, then work up a lather between my hands. The soap's woodsy masculine scent is heaven. Asher's eyes open and he looks so surprised when I gently spread the suds over his chest, begin washing his skin, taking care of him first. Because of the way he tenses, I don't think anyone has in the past.

Let me be the one to give him the feeling of loving touch over and over then.

"What should I do?" His gravelly voice competes to be heard above the water spray.

By what I read in his eyes, he's eager to please me, uncomfortable being first.

"You can touch me," I begin my consent. "There is not

one ounce of me that doesn't believe that however you touch me won't feel good. But for right now, let's just shower and get clean. Get to know each other this way."

When I finish washing him, he begins, with shaky, soapy hands, to explore my body, asking if it's okay before touching my breasts, my ass, between my thighs. With each 'yes' I give, I'm rewarded with worshipping touch.

He asks about the blue morpho butterfly tattoo on my back spanning shoulder blade to shoulder blade, identical to the one on November's back. And I tell him about seeing butterflies after my father died, and how November saw them after the death of her parents, her brother. Asher asks about the 11:11 tattoo on the back of my neck, and I tell him about angel numbers and manifestation. He asks about the 'Love you' tattoos in different handwriting on my inner wrists. I hesitate for a few seconds before giving him my answer because I wonder if it's a reminder that he never had the love of parents.

After each tattoo is rinsed, he places a reverent kiss on my skin in the same place.

By the time I'm washed clean, Asher's hands are steady.

I've read hundreds of romance novels. *Thousands?* Wouldn't surprise me. The way Asher is talking to me, the way he's touching me, I feel like the FMC in the very best type of spicy scene. Asher may not have had a lot of sex in his life, but he absolutely knows what he's doing. From the moment he carried me from the bathroom and laid me down on his bed, my skin buzzed with the anticipation of something deliciously good coming my way.

He hovers over me, propped up on his hands, his cock hot and heavy against my inner thigh, pre-cum wetting my damp skin, dark eyes hooded as they drink me in. He watches the movement of my hands skimming my breasts, giving my nipples a pinch before moving down my belly to stroke my fingers across my clit, feeling how drenched I've become and it's not water from the shower.

Asher shifts his weight to one arm, then takes my slick fingers into his mouth to taste me, eyes closing, throat humming with satisfaction. His mouth is warm, his tongue teasing as he sucks my coated fingers. My pussy clenches tight, and I think I may have become impossibly wetter. I didn't know what to expect from Asher during sex, but I know not that!

I ease my fingers from his mouth, wrap my hand around the nape of his neck, feeling the wet ends of his hair, and pull him in for a deep kiss. It's an instantly hot, needy mess. When we break, he's breathing hard, but so am I.

"I . . . I . . ." His brain is short circuiting. "I want to do so much to you, but I don't think I can last the first time. Maybe not even the second."

His cheeks redden with embarrassment; I will not allow him to feel less than by what is out of his control.

"Then I suggest we get one of those new condoms on you, and I'll show you the quickest way to my orgasm while you're inside me."

He groans, stretches his arm to the nightstand, and retrieves a box from the top drawer as my hands stroke his ribcage, his back, his firm ass. He groans again, and I feel more pre-cum leak against my abdomen this time. I take the box from him and rip it open as he presses his lips to mine, parting them with his tongue, and explores my mouth the way his cock might want to explore my pussy. It's sexy and arousing and I fumble with the condom wrapper until Asher breaks the kiss, takes it from me, and finishes the task.

Asher hovers close above me, forehead resting against

my shoulder as his knee spreads my legs a bit wider, creating room for his hips. He lifts his head to look me in my eyes, adoration and a question as he lines the tip of his cock at my entrance.

"Please, Asher."

He slowly thrusts inside before I finish saying his name.

The stretch around him feels so right, so mind-shattering good even though he isn't able to enter me all the way. It takes a few thrusts for me to take him in fully, both of us moaning in unison, skin turning hot as we slide against each other.

We are learning each other in a whole new, wonderful way.

"Tell me what to do," he shakily commands.

I guide his fingers down to my clit and show him how to rub me there. I didn't expect it to be, but it's good from first touch. Asher pays attention to the details, and the way he shifts his pelvis to rub against mine every time he plunges deep, makes my body quake. This . . . This . . . This gets Asher going and he fucks me faster, sure to hit that spot every time. He moves his hand around to my ass, grabs my flesh, and hauls my hips up to him. He's barely pulling back before thrusting again, fast and deep. The friction. The depth. The grind.

I cry out. His cry picks up where I left off.

My pussy contracts, and I feel him pulse through his orgasm inside me. The weight of his shaking body. His arms tight around me, face buried in my neck, breathing in clean sweat, his soap, and the essence of me. And I of him.

Asher knows himself; he doesn't last long the second time, yet makes sure I come seconds before he does. But after a short nap, I straddle him and he takes me in long, deep thrusts over and over, sucks and nips on my nipples until they are painfully tight and makes me come before tossing me on my back to fuck me hard into the mattress. I come again, long before it's his turn. And I get to watch him unravel in pleasure.

When Bisou and Jin awaken and whine to be let out of their pen, we reluctantly slip out of bed. Asher pulls a white T-shirt from his top dresser drawer and, grudgingly, dresses me in it. It hangs almost to my knees, covering me entirely, but when Asher's eyes laser focus on my nipples poking the soft cotton, his dick starts getting hard. He reaches for me, but I step back.

"We walk the dogs, eat dinner, then you can do filthy things to me."

His sigh is heavy with disappointment, but he dresses in jeans and a T-shirt, slips on brown flip flops, then harnesses up the puppies for their walk. I slip next door to pull on a casual halter dress I don't have to wear a bra or panties with; fewer items to take off later, then begin making a meal of fettuccini with chicken and asparagus which we eat on the balcony.

We end the evening at my place, in my bed, making slow love before turning off the lights and settling in for a good night's sleep.

"Genevieve?" Asher's voice is low and sleepy.

"Hm?"

"Can I sleep close to you? Hold you?"

"Is that how you usually sleep with someone?"

"I've never held anyone while sleeping."

"But you want to try?"

"With you, yes. But if that makes you uncomfortable, I understand."

"No. It's just, I've never been held while sleeping."

There's a pause before he asks, "How is that possible?"

"Haven't a clue." I giggle lazily.

"May I hold you?"

I smile. "Please, do."

Asher becomes the big spoon flush against my little spoon, slipping one arm under my pillow, his other around my ribcage and up my chest for me to hold. It's warm, seamless, comforting.

Perfection.

Asher

Without his glasses, Asher can see, but everything is a little hazy. His other senses are more than fine. He can still smell the fragrance of Genevieve's hair, the scent of her warm skin. He can still taste her sweet lips, discover the flavors of the hills and valleys and plains of her skin, the hot slick between her legs. He can still feel her nipples harden under the pinch of his fingertips, feel the effect her naked body has when pressed against his, feel her heart race with his own. Asher can still hear when . . . What has he seen in a few of the romance novels he's read recently? He can still hear the sounds his Genevieve makes when she 'tips over the edge . . .'

Chapter Twenty-Two

GENEVIEVE

Are my feet touching the ground?

After two days holed up in either Asher's apartment or mine, I feel completely blissed out: happier than I've ever been in my adult life.

Last night, we slept at Asher's. We figured it would be easier for me to slip out while the puppies slept and get ready at my place for a long day of employee interviews. But it wasn't the puppies who had a difficult time letting me go. Asher, half asleep, kept whispering in my ear "One more minute" as he held me tight. Honestly, I didn't want to leave his bed. The warmth and comfort of his limbs wrapped around me felt too good, but I have business to attend to—damn adulting!

By the time I park in front of my bookstore at a quarter to eight, I see November's car already parked at the curb. Dressed in a cornflower blue blouse, black pencil skirt, and black peep-toe pumps, she steps out of her black Mercedes, a gift from Rhys, and greets me on the sidewalk with a big hug. I feel like I haven't seen her in ages even though I saw her on Sunday, but a lot has happened since then.

November breaks the hug, places a hand on each of my shoulders, and gives me a good once over.

"Well, Gen, don't you look all glowy. How is Asher doing?" she knowingly inquires.

"Well, Em, my boyfriend-"

"Boyfriend?" she squeals, her eyes wide with excitement.

"Yes, Asher asked if I would be his girlfriend."

Even though we're both wearing high heels, we manage to mock jump up and down, holding onto each other's arms.

"That's too adorable!" Em exclaims. "I totally see him being so polite in asking. When did this happen?"

We calm down but still hold onto each other.

"Monday," I answer.

Her eyebrows shoot upward. "And it took you two days to tell me?"

"I wanted to tell you in person."

"Oh, please!" She rolls her eyes. "You and your *boyfriend* were canoodling for the last two days."

There is no way I can beat back my giddiness, and it shows.

"And for how glowy you are, I gather the canoodling is five stars."

Happy tears prick behind my eyes. "More like all the stars in the sky."

November turns serious. "He's good to you."

"So much more than good."

My best friend hugs me again and says, "Then he is exactly who I want for you."

I break the hug before I might really cry; I don't want to be red and blotchy for the interviews. I bend my elbow and point a thumb toward the bookstore entrance.

"Do you mind a quick peek inside before we head up to the conference room? I just want to check the progress."

"Ooooooo! I want to see!"

When we step inside, I am beyond impressed. The shelving units throughout the store have been installed and painted since I was last here. There are no workers to be seen. No James. And other than Asher refinishing the cashier counter, this stage of the workplan might be complete.

"Gen! This is farther along than I expected." November's voice sounds wonder-struck, her eyes darting around.

"Funny thing . . ." I start before telling her about Asher owning the building.

"Rhys never told me, but I don't think I told him that Asher is the one to find the space for you. I think I only said you found a location during a phone call when he was on a work trip. I had no idea. I mean, I know Asher does well for himself, but I didn't know how well."

"I get it. Asher is humble about everything." We turn and head toward the back exit that leads to the building's main lobby. "Did you know Gareth lives in the penthouse apartment here?"

"I knew he moved recently to a building with a waterfront view, but he hasn't invited us over yet. Maybe we should 'Ding, Dong, Ditch' him before we leave for the day."

This makes me laugh out loud as I lock the door behind us.

Our first two interviews of the day are a bust. One young man, who applied to work the bookstore side, wants to start as a manager of the store, knows nothing about romance books, nor reading from what November and I can tell. This isn't my first rodeo. I know the ups and downs of the interview process having done this in my previous job. November, who works for herself as a successful wellness coach, is flabbergasted that he had the audacity to apply. The other person interviewed is a reader but didn't realize this is an all-romance bookstore, and it's not a genre for her.

We have better luck when Lucy, the property management office receptionist, walks in wearing a white button-down shirt, gray slacks, and black loafers. Turns out, Lucy is a romance reader with a special place in her heart for hockey romances, Denise Williams, B.K. Borison, and Lynn Painter.

When I ask Lucy about her current office position, she explains, "My training rotation period in the office ends soon. To be honest, Mr. Sinclair encouraged me to apply for this job and my advisors helped me with my resume and coached me in mock interviews."

November, who I pre-informed about the need to hire at least one young adult from Perseverance, and I exchange a quick, nonverbal conversation, and I hire Lucy on the spot. The very young woman looks like she might cry at landing a job she is excited to work.

"Thank you! I can't believe it! I will make sure you will never regret giving me a chance!" She stands and profusely shakes my hand, then November's.

November and I both have to glue ourselves to our chairs, because if we stand, we will hug Lucy and hugging would be unprofessional. When Lucy leaves, we stand and do a little jig in our heels.

We get through the remainder of the interviews for the book side of the store before our lunch break at the little French café on the other side of the building. Excluding Lucy, there were four candidates who stood out, but I only have three remaining positions to fill. November and I break it down over grilled salmon and asparagus with a lemon sauce.

As November brings a forkful of salmon to her mouth, she asks, "How much did you love Lucas' answer to why does he read romance novels?"

"He's a genius boy in wanting to know what women want." I finish my chuckle before sipping from my glass of sparkling water.

November swallows and forks asparagus next. "God, he actually blushed. And when he said he got hooked on the heart of the writing . . ."

"I'm hiring him, you know."

"Oh, I know. I'd be so mad if you didn't."

"Soooooo mad."

We're sitting at a sidewalk bistro table for two. The sun is high above, bright, but not annoying considering I forgot my sunglasses in the car. It's just a few short days until June, and it hits me that my bookstore will be opening in just a few short weeks.

"Can you believe I'm actually doing this?" The question is meant to stay in my head, but my mouth has a mind of its own.

"I can." November sets her fork down, tines resting on the rim of her plate. "And it's going to be great."

After lunch, interviews for the coffee bar begin. November and I skim over the application of the first candidate who has great experience working as a barista in Rome and Manhattan. On paper, Astrid, the candidate's first name, reads exactly what I'm looking for creating bookish specialty drinks.

There's a knock on the conference room door.

I call out, "Come in!"

November's eyebrows furrow and I hear her murmur, "Astrid?"

But November is looking at her tablet and not the nearly six feet, willowy woman who just stepped into the room who looks vaguely familiar to me. It's her height and her straight, partially white, partially light gold blonde hair that stands out to me, but I can't place her.

November looks up from the tablet and repeats herself, "Astrid?"

"November?" Astrid looks equally bewildered.

I have no idea what's going on, but I stand and extend my right hand to Astrid. "Hi Astrid, I'm Genevieve Torres. I guess you already know November Day. Please, have a seat."

November speaks to me but doesn't take her eyes off Astrid. "Astrid currently works for Alex at A New Day."

The pieces fall into place. One or two times per week, I take Pilates classes at November's sister-in-law's studio. I must have seen Astrid there in passing.

Astrid's big blue eyes somehow become larger. "I think I should start by telling you, Alex knows I'm applying for this position. I want more hours and A New Day is fully staffed." She looks to me. "In your advertisement, you stated the lead barista position will work Monday through Friday. Alex said if I'm hired, I can stay on at A New Day and work a few hours on the weekends as needed. I love Alex and working at her studio, but I really need more hours."

"Alex didn't tell me you were applying here," November states. "Then again, she probably didn't know I was helping Genevieve with interviews."

"I asked Alex not to say anything, and I didn't know you would be here either. I want to get hired because I'm a fantastic barista. I may not have done this type of work in a while, but I guarantee, my skills are intact. The bonus is: I'm an avid reader of contemporary romance and romantasy."

I already like Astrid. I like her confidence. She may not smile, but I don't feel her to be unkind. I happen to know a man who isn't big on smiling, at least until he met me, who is the best kind of person.

I look to November, who gives me a slight head nod, then back to Astrid.

"Okay, Astrid. Let's chat."

Steak for dinner? Did Bisou do okay without me?

Steak =  Bisou is fine if she has one parent around.

I appreciate you so much.

How much?

A two-word loaded question that turns me on high. I sink my teeth into my bottom lip.

I guess I'll have to show you . . .

Gareth is here. Let's see if I can kick him out.

Rude!

He's been working here most of the day.

Is that usual?

No.

Be home in 10. Missed you!

Missed you more!

The scene I walk into is more than funny.

Gareth, in light gray office attire sans jacket, has made himself at home on the couch. Jin and Bisou are sitting on the cushion beside him, enraptured by the way Gareth speaks to them about how lucky they are to be living the spoiled puppy life. Meanwhile, he pays zero attention to my glowering boyfriend who stands in the middle of the room with his arms folded across his chest.

If I was a stranger, I would never guess these two men are, essentially, best friends.

"Hi, all!" I say to the room.

Bisou and Jin are beside themselves with joy that I'm home; this may not be my apartment, but it feels like home. The puppies trample over Gareth's lap to get to the end of the long couch closest to me, still scared to jump off on their own.

My tone slides to baby talk as I greet my precious furballs, petting them as they lick my hands. "Hello! Hi, my precious babies! I missed you so much. Hi! Hi! Such the cutest puppies in the world. Yes, you are. Hi!"

Asher approaches slowly, giving me time with the kids, but I know he wants me in his arms. His emotions practically vibrate off him.

Gareth stands. "What fickle friends your dogs are!"

"They just know who's closest to their hearts," I comment, continuing to pet the puppies. "You could adopt your own, you know."

"As tempting as that might be, I'm not home enough. I couldn't offer the stability the two of you do."

There's no teasing tone, and that's what makes me look up. I see a glimpse of something, a longing that quickly disappears behind the playboy bachelor façade again.

"Would you like to stay for dinner, Gareth?" I ask, meaning it.

I think I sense Asher's entire body tense.

"Thank you, but no." I think Gareth felt it too. "If I stay, Asher may stab me with his steak knife."

I laugh, but Asher doesn't. I understand it to mean Gareth has been annoying him all the workday. I pick up Jin and place her in Dad's arms, then pick up Bisou and snuggle her.

Nice dress be damned!

"Then, would you be interested in attending a coffee tasting?" I ask. "I hired a lead barista today who will be creating specialty drinks for the coffee bar. She has a great resume."

"Count me in. I should get to know the staff since I plan to pick up my daily coffee in your establishment. Love that a coffee bar moved into my building." Gareth picks up his jacket from the back of the couch and slings it over his shoulder before picking up his work bag. "I'm also kind of curious to see what all this romance fuss is about. I'll consider it a comparative study. Me versus men in books. I already know I'll win."

My eyeball roll is accompanied by an eyebrow raise. "I'll text you the details when I have them. Are you sure you won't stay for dinner?"

Gareth looks to Asher, then back to me. "Positive."

I don't know what possesses me, but I hand Bisou to Asher and give Gareth a quick, completely platonic hug goodbye that takes Gareth by surprise. It's over in a blink, and Gareth begins his walk down the hall but stops and turns around.

"I see why you're the best thing that has ever happened to him, Genevieve. You're good for my friend. You make a difference. I'm happy for you both. Truly." I may not know him well, but I know Gareth doesn't hold back. He's only been honest with me, so his words mean something.

Asher places our puppies back on the couch, then comes to stand behind me, wraps his arms around my waist, holding me close as we watch Gareth exit the apartment.

I am overwhelmed, grateful to have found a home full of love.

Asher

Asher wakes and his first thought is of her. It feels like every third thought he has is of her. When he's working out. When he's in the shower; perhaps more in here, if he's being honest. When he's working, Asher notices certain tasks are taking a little longer than usual because he's clock-watching, counting down the hours, minutes, and seconds until he can be with Genevieve again.

He sleeps and dreams of her.

She's distracting . . .

Asher welcomes it.

Chapter Twenty-Three

GENEVIEVE

Years ago, when I started planning for opening an all-romance bookstore and café, the plan was to open in Los Angeles during autumn. I thought it would be fun to open during my favorite season, dress up the store in all the fall colors, and build a fanbase in time for the holidays. My dream is coming to fruition with a few changes including the store opening on the first day of summer, and in Buffalo. So, the fall décor and beverages and displays are placed on hold for now, and I'm creating a whole new look for summer with beach reads and more iced beverages on the menu. Actually, Astrid is handling that menu.

After a couple opening conversations with Astrid about my expectations of her role in Mine's coffee bar, I swiftly understand she possesses knowledge of the coffee business that far exceed my own; I am a novice compared to her. Acknowledging this leads me to, one, change her title from Lead Barista to Beverage Innovator. She is the only employee who started work this week, assisting me with equipment ordering and setup, purchasing supplies, creating a training plan for the baristas (two young men from the Perseverance program), and creating the coffee bar menu including contracting with a popular local bakery for the baked goods to be offered at Mine. Astrid is a dream and I'm counting my lucky stars in finding her. The first five days of her employment have eased my mind that the coffee bar is being taken good care of.

It's happening.

I can handle the next two weeks until grand opening in one of two ways: one) revel in my dream becoming a reality, or, two) spiral into sheer panic. If this past week is any indication, I will ping pong between both sides.

Now that the construction is complete and the bookstore is safe, I have brought Bisou to the bookstore every day this week; Jin a couple days in a row when Asher had to work at Morgan Security. He would have taken Jin with him, since Rhys' assistant, Sophie, LOVES Jin, but I like Bisou to have company while I work at the bookstore.

I sit at one of the recently delivered marble top bistro tables situated away from the other coffee bar seating, closer to the bookstore side of the retail space. This table has its own window, not as large as the other windows, yet enough of a sliver to allow a little bit of the outside world in, enough room for one person to spread out a bit, yet cozy for two to share hot coffee and warm almond croissants in the morning before delving into their workdays.

As I sit here, waiting for a couple more furniture deliveries, I receive a text from my love.

> If I work faster, I can be out of here in an
> hour. Problem is, I keep thinking of you.

Thump, thump, thump–goes my heart.

Thinking of what we did last night? Or
about what we will be doing tonight?

I have no regrets, but I should never have
started putting my hands on you.

Hands on me? Do you mean fucking me?

I was trying not to use that word.

Why? It's a great word.

Using that word makes things happen in
context to you that I can't control.

Who knew I would ever get to text like this with intro-
verted Asher Adams? I laugh.

Are you talking about your dick getting
hard?

You need to stop. I was only texting to
ask if I should meet you at the shop or at
home.

Text me when you're done. I'll meet you
at home after the last deliveries.

And why stop? Are you getting hard
again?

Getting? I've been hard on and off all day.
I can't stop thinking about you.

My nipples stiffen; my core pulses.
Maybe I shouldn't have started this, but . . .

> You could have fucked your fist in the
> shower this morning to take the edge off.

I did since you were already gone before I
woke up.

Love his honesty!

> Want to share what you were thinking
> about in the shower?

Filthy things.

> Details!

My greedy eyes hover over my cell phone watching the
text bubbles.

You joined me in the shower. Saw me
stroking myself. Slid to your knees and
took me into your mouth.

That's definitely something I would do. *Hmmm . . .*

> Did I work your cock? Or did you fuck my
> mouth? Either way, did you call me a
> good girl for taking your big hard cock so
> well?

Christ! Stepping away from the
phone now.

When Asher texts me he's on his way home, I'm in the
middle of receiving numerous furniture and product deliveries. Saddle brown leather armchairs, hunter green perfor-
mance velvet loveseats, and a variety of small coffee and side

tables arrive for the coffee bar. The pantry cabinet I bought for the wall behind the cashier counter is delivered and will be used for storage in the lower solid doored portion, extra counter space, and displays behind the upper windowed doors. Nadia, the woman I contracted to create a trope candle line for Mine, stops by to deliver the merchandise, and it all turned out better than I hoped. After she leaves, I place one of the vanilla sandalwood *Slow Burn* candles into my tote to take home to Asher, and one cinnamon amber *He Falls First* candle for November, because Rhys definitely fell first.

Jin and Bisou are more than ready to go home by the time everyone leaves. They are barely able to stand still while I place the harnesses and leashes on them. I don't blame them; it has been a longer than usual day at the bookstore and, like them, I miss their dad. I text Asher we are on our way home, and he hearts the message. One last walk through the store, turning off lights along the way, I am itching to start stocking the shelves, but that begins on Monday. Leashes in hand, heavy tote bag on my shoulder, I set the alarm, lock the door, and head home in the breezy late afternoon.

The entire twenty-minute door-to-door commute, I think about my text exchange with Asher, and I can't remember ever having this extreme attraction to a man before. Of course, I've been turned on by men, but not nearly like this. With Asher, it's more than him being handsome. His heart is like no other I have ever known. If I want to know what he's thinking and feeling, he will lower his walls and let me in. The way he looks at me, his eyes warm with love, my heart is overwhelmed, reshaped into a vessel that can hold more.

By the time my car is parked, things and puppies gathered, and I step onto the elevator, every inch of my skin is vibrating. My nipples are so sensitized, the satin of my bra is too much. I can't imagine if I had worn a lace one. And I'm trying to ignore the slip and slide in my panties as I walk-pathetically wet! The elevator's soft ding snaps me out of my sex-hazed brain, and I step forward as the door slides open, but I can't step off because of the tall body blocking my way.

Asher looks . . . crazed. His hair is messy as if he's had his hands tugging in it all day. The beautiful green, gold, and brown of his irises have been swallowed by his pupils. His teeth worry his plump bottom lip. My eyes dip down to the bulging outline at the front of his jeans, and I shiver all over, feeling like prey trapped in a cage with a starving panther. Scared? No. I want this panther to devour me.

My eyes meet his focused stare. "Hey."

"Hey." His voice is hot desert sand and I am his cool glass of water.

The elevator door attempts to slide closed, but Asher's hand comes down fast to stop it. He stands aside to allow me off, taking the tote bag from my shoulder as I pass, and, finally, greets the puppies, scooping up Jin with one hand as we walk. He holds her to his chest and talks to her in sweet tones, telling her, "Yes, I missed you too."

"What if it was someone else in the elevator?" I ask as I pick up Bisou so she doesn't feel left out.

"Explode into a million pieces. Rip the building apart with my bare hands." He places Jin back on the ground as he pulls his keys out of his pocket and unlocks my front door.

"So, violence," I say as my teasing fingers brush his denim-covered erection as I pass by and enter my apartment.

He sets my tote down on the floor in front of the coat closet, then sets the puppies free of their harnesses and doesn't watch them scamper to the living room, because his dark eyes are hyper-focused on me.

My back is against the wall before my blink is complete.

Asher braces himself with one hand on the wall, the other firm on my hip.

"You teased me mercilessly all day long," he growls.

My fingers take a stroll up his abdomen. "It was one text conversation."

"I know, but in my head . . ." He shuts his eyes tight. "You were there. You're always there."

My hands grab hold of the front of his marine blue Henley, pull him down to me, but I don't kiss him passionately the way I want to. No, I kiss him firmly, lips to lips. I break the kiss and wrap my arms tight around his neck, our bodies flush. Me being on his mind all day wasn't just about sex. I feel a lightbulb switch on in my head, a bright, shining light of comprehension.

All these deep feelings I have for Asher, I know how to process them because I have had a life of people I love and who love me back. It may not be romantic love, but love nonetheless. For Asher, this truly is an awakening, and my heart equally breaks under the weight of sadness and bursts with joy. I may not understand how at thirty years old I am his first and, hopefully, last love, and there are devastating thoughts about never feeling love that I won't allow to seep into my brain because it no longer matters. I am here. I am his. He is mine. None of the before is relevant to this moment of being in each other's arms. This I understand.

"I missed you today, Asher." I squeeze him, because, maybe, I can press my meaning into his body. "I miss you every time we're apart because you are my heart."

We are alike in this.

Asher holds me so close; I don't know where I begin or he ends.

Let me be the one . . .

Asher

Asher can't stop shaking his head in disbelief. For the first time in his life, he feels like he belongs. Everything good he's done in his life has been tallied and he's been given a gift he never dared hope for. All the birthdays never acknowledged, all the holidays unobserved, made up for. For the first time in his life, Asher feels he matters.

Chapter Twenty-Four

GENEVIEVE

"Is this going to work? You are so much taller than I am."

"Trust me, Genevieve. I am highly motivated to be inside you."

The laugh I release is stifled by the linen sheets, but the moment Asher pushes into my pussy, my laugh turns to a low moan.

My pillow and his are currently under my pelvis. Engineer that he is, he worked the problem and came up with a solution. We tried doggy-style early on, but it was just awkward and uncomfortable, and we moved onto something else that felt much more satisfying. Something new I've learned about Asher: he doesn't give up easily. I'm sure this specific dedication is his desire to explore my body in every way a million times, but I'm hoping that dedication to find a solution lends itself to other areas of our relationship, especially when we eventually argue.

"Asher!" A muffled cry escapes me.

I prop up on my elbows and twist to look over my shoulder at what Asher is doing to me that feels intensely good. I feel myself become wetter, nipples tighter, mouth dryer at the sight of him straddling my legs, hands grabbing the mounds of my ass, as he watches his hard, hot cock disappear inside my pussy. He's naked and beautiful and mine.

I reach a hand to one of his, holding tight to his wrist. His eyes dart to mine and hold, fucking me deeper as I clench around him. Both of us moan in unison.

"I'm so close." Something about this position; he's hitting all the right spots all at once.

"I feel it. Come for me, Genevieve." His voice is hot and pleading.

And, by whomever runs this universe, I come on Asher's command.

I was going to indulge in that fantasy of his, going down on him in the shower, but Asher doesn't like the idea of not being able to reciprocate and that would make us late this morning. Late wouldn't be a good look to host my own coffee tasting. Instead, Asher hoists me up his body, pins me against the cold marble wall, and this hard, deep quickie strikes gold. I wonder if he has secret schematics of my body in his computer . . .

I'm still buzzing from sex endorphins when we walk through the entrance of Mine. We left Bisou and Jin together at Asher's, because we do need to start leaving them alone. This tasting is the perfect opportunity; it will only be about an hour, then Asher will go home to work. He was apprehensive over leaving them alone, and I think that's why he was so quiet on the drive here.

"Wow! The coffee bar setup looks fantastic," Asher comments.

As we walk to the bar, I have to admit, without criticism, it does. The browns and greens mixed with the warm brass hardware accents blend seamlessly, are inviting, and exactly the feel I wanted in this space. I want customers to come in and want to linger. And to add to the ambience, my favorite smell in the world: freshly brewing coffee.

"Good morning, Astrid!" I exclaim.

Astrid is wearing her white blonde hair pulled into a severe high ponytail, accentuating her high cheekbones and straight nose. She looks like a fae character who walked right out of a fantasy novel. She looks up and gives me a small, yet warm, smile that defies her cool façade.

"Good morning, Boss Lady!"

"You are too funny." I wrap my arm around Asher's and I feel his tension. "Astrid Collins, I would like you to meet my significant other, Asher Adams. You'll be seeing Asher here quite a bit, probably working on his laptop or reading."

I feel his tension morph into relief, and I think Asher wasn't clear on who we were to be to each other at my bookstore.

Asher extends his right hand to Astrid. "Nice to meet you. Genevieve told me about your skillset, and I know you will be an asset here."

"Nice to meet you too, and thank you." Astrid shakes his hand and releases it. "I know I'm going to love working here. I get to be creative in a book environment. What's not to love?"

"Asher refinished this bar and the cashier counter himself," I gush.

"Then it's you I need to thank for my magnificent workstation. It's truly the most beautiful bar I have had the pleasure to work at."

"Thank you." He doesn't shy away from the compliment, but I can tell he's uncomfortable.

"Do you need any help setting up?" I ask Astrid.

"I have everything under control."

"Great! I'm going to show Asher around and wait for our guests to arrive."

Astrid returns to her measurements, equipment, and concoctions, looking like the alchemist she is.

I take Asher by the hand and lead him back toward the entrance and beyond.

"We have a little time before everyone arrives. Would you like me to help move some boxes for you?" he asks. "You haven't shown me how you laid out the bookstore sections yet, will you give me the tour?"

"All that can wait. I want to show you something else."

Asher takes in the little corner table by the narrow window I led him to. Instead of the other round bistro tables in the coffee bar, I opted for a square one in the same style because this allows a little more surface space to work. There are still only two chairs here, but I added hunter green velvet seat pads for comfort. Two table height brass stanchions stand sentry, joined together by a velvet rope the same color as the seat pads. A very fancy gold-tone picture frame set horizontally at the middle of the table reads 'Reserved for Asher & Genevieve.'

"What's this?" he asks in nearly a whisper.

"This table is just for our use. I thought anytime you want to come in for a change in scenery to work, you could sit here. If we just want to be alone, this is where we'll sit. No one else is allowed here."

Before I know what's happening, Asher hauls me into his arms and plants an all-consuming kiss on my lips. It's pure passion; lips, tongue, and teeth. It's his heart filling with cups of newly found goodness. It's thank you, thank you, thank you.

"Oh my gosh! This lovey-dovey vibe is everything right now!"

We break apart at the sound of November's giddy voice, and turn around to see her with her sister-in-law, Alex; both amused eyes and wide toothy grins. Rhys stands a few feet behind them looking anywhere but at me and Asher.

I'm not embarrassed by PDA, but Asher might . . . I glance up to him and his swollen lips, but he looks fine with the attention. He didn't even take one step away from me.

More walls of Asher crumbling down.

"Hi! Welcome!" I exclaim, and give a round of hugs, including Rhys who has made his way over to the group. "I am so glad you all could come. Alex, thank you."

"Me being here is twofold. Of course, I want to get a sneak peek at your new business, so I can shout it to my clients, but I also want to support Astrid in her new endeavor. This job means the world to her. I hope you know that."

"I so appreciate you, Alex. I'm lucky to have Astrid here." I may not know Alex well, and I will make time to do so, but I have always liked her. She has this new life but has always made it point to stay close to November, still treating her like a true sister after the death of her first husband, November's brother, Roman. "Come on, let's get this show on the road."

My guests walk across the store, oohing and ahhing at what they see along the way. The store may not be complete, but it's still music to my ears. We pony up to the bar; me at one end, then Asher, November, Rhys, then Alex. Funny it ended up boy, girl, boy, girl.

I sense someone approach the bar, feel a hand on my shoulder. Asher and I twist at the waist to see Gareth has arrived.

"Sorry I'm late, but it's so early." He leans in to place a kiss on my cheek, keeping it quick as to not annoy Asher.

I pat his arm. "Lucky for you, you're about to have a serious amount of caffeine."

"It's never enough."

There's an echo to Gareth's words. No, it's Astrid speaking the identical words at nearly the same time. Their eyes meet, flash, and it's obvious they are familiar with each other.

Please don't let Astrid be one of Gareth's hookups.

"I must be still in bed and dreaming, because how are you here?" Gareth asks, but it's . . . odd wording.

"I work here," Astrid replies, looking incredulous.

He folds his arms across his chest. "No, you work at A New Day."

"Yes. I work here too."

"Why?" Gareth sounds irritated.

Astrid shakes her head to show it's beneath her to answer. Without paying any more attention to Gareth, she begins, and Gareth takes the empty seat next to Alex.

"Good morning, I'm Astrid, your Beverage Innovator. I'm excited to present to you a sampling of what Mine will offer its customers once we open." Astrid looks down the line of her guests. Her smile falters to a near grimace when her eyes meet Gareth's but returns when she looks back to the rest of us. "We can't possibly taste everything on the menu, so I pulled a few specialty drinks for you to choose from. First, we'll start with a tea flight." She gestures to the individual rectangular boards with small Moroccan tea glasses in pink, green, and gold.

"I thought I was here for a coffee tasting," Gareth snarks.

Astrid ignores him. "The tea served at Mine comes from this great woman-owned company located in the

Hudson Valley called Warm Heart. The tea makers buy and grow fresh fruits and herbs, then dry and sachet the combinations themselves. This morning, we are sampling three of my favorite herbal blends. I stuck with decaf because of the espresso-based drinks we will be tasting next."

"Thank God," Gareth grumbles.

"In the pink glass, we have a blend of hibiscus, berries and rose. In the green glass, peppermint softened with vanilla and cornflower. In the gold, saffron, lemon, and ginger."

My guests, including Gareth, begin to pick up the warm glasses and sniff the fragrances and take sips.

"Oh, this hibiscus one is delicious!" Alex exclaims. "Does Warm Heart sell boxes online?"

I lean forward to see Alex down the bar, standing between Gareth and Rhys. "Yes, but for your convenience, we will be selling boxes of the teas we serve in store."

"Good marketing," Rhys comments.

"I'd be ignorant to think my customers will come in for every cup of tea they drink, so they can still support Mine and Warm Heart by taking a box home. And, by the way, these tea and coffee flights will be on the menu."

"Served hot or iced," Astrid adds.

Asher places a hand on my back and rubs up and down; his sweet, silent way to show he's proud of me, then snakes his arm around my waist, his thumb finds and strokes my skin under my red T-shirt just above the waistband of my jeans. I practically melt under the touch.

As the group sip tea, makes commentary about the flavors and the coffee bar decor, Astrid prepares the coffee flights.

"You like to touch me," I whisper to Asher.

"I like to know you're here. I like to know you're mine."

He lightly presses his lips to my temple, then catches my eye. "I hope it's not too clingy."

I place my hand against his chest, over his heart. "Don't you dare stop touching me, because I love the feeling of being wanted, of being yours."

Out of the corner of my eye, I see Rhys approach. Asher notices too because he turns his attention away from me. Rhys is staring at his cell phone, reading a text or maybe an email.

"Sorry to interrupt," Rhys says to me before looking to Asher. "I just received a text from Sophie to check my emails. Looks like the last of the equipment for the I-Core Devices build in Silicon Valley arrives on Friday. Per our contract, wheels up on Sunday."

Asher's face falls. "That's earlier than anticipated. I thought it would be another two weeks."

Rhys cocks his head to the side, expression serious, no, concerned, but says nothing.

"That's an eight-day project." Asher runs his hand through his hair. "The bookstore's grand opening is next week on Saturday."

Understanding dawns on Rhys' face, then sympathy. "If I could, I would do it alone, but it would take too many days beyond what has been agreed upon."

Confused, I look between Asher and Rhys. "What's going on?"

November, who has been listening, has come over to stand by Rhys, placing a hand on his back.

Asher turns fully to me, taking my hands in his, and the look in his eyes is pure disappointment. More like he's disappointing me and hates himself for it.

"Genevieve, I have to go out of town for this job. I agreed to it long before . . ."

"Gen, you know I plan to help out opening week,"

November chimes in. "With all the employees working, we will get everything done. The grand opening will be spectacular. Smooth sailing all the way."

"Yes. Of course. We have plenty of staff. No worries."

I place my everything-is-okay mask on, but the way November's eyebrows furrow, she knows I feel like crying but doesn't dare give me away.

Yes, everything will get done; that is not my concern. I've always managed to stay on point with large-scale projects and the details needing to be handled. What I'm masking is not having Asher here to come home to, to hold me at night, to soothe away my worries. I already told my family not to come see the store until after the opening, because it will be too busy and I won't have time to entertain them beforehand. I can't put my disappointment front and center, because I know what it will do to Asher.

I keep my mask on, and tell Asher, "It will be perfectly okay. We'll make plans tonight."

He does not look reassured.

Asher

This past week began on such a high note: Genevieve told Asher she loves him. Yet, since Tuesday, Asher has felt a slide backwards, insecurity creeping in. He understands this is in no way anyone's fault, but he still curses his bad luck. To combat that insecurity, all he can do is work his ass off to make sure Genevieve has everything she needs while he's away, so she still loves him when he returns. Yes, he knows it's an insane thought process, but it's all he has.

Chapter Twenty-Five

GENEVIEVE

When Sunday morning arrives, I'm relieved. Even though Asher leaves for California today, I'm glad the day is finally here so we can stop walking on eggshells over it. I'm not looking forward to saying goodbye to him for eight days, but I'm glad to be done with the anxious anticipation of his departure. Since we received the bad news on Tuesday, Asher has been over-compensating like this is his fault, no matter how I tell him otherwise. (Poor Rhys! November told me how upset he was and how he tried to find a loophole in the contract.)

All week, he has been bending over backwards prepping for his trip in addition to other work he has but also spending time at the store with me: unpacking boxes; shelving books; assisting me with creating a cash register and timecard training guide for my new employees–none of which he has to do. I didn't feel I could refuse his help because he feels terrible he won't be here for one of the most important days of my life.

In the middle of Saturday night, after Asher passed out from sheer exhaustion, I sneak out of his bed and go to my apartment to make lemon streusel muffins, the first food I ever made for him, and while they bake, I have a good cry to take the edge off my stress over the week ahead. And for being without Asher. Logically, I know my tears are nonsensical, but the heart wants what it wants.

When there are no more tears to wring out of me, I wash my face, place eye patches fresh from the refrigerator under my eyes, then return to Asher's apartment. I place the boxed muffins in his packed suitcase and slip a paperback copy of *Love and Other Conspiracies* by Mallory Marlowe in his carry-on luggage. On my way back to Asher's bedroom, I glance at the sleeping puppies.

Jin is going to miss . . .

I can't even allow that thought to creep in and take hold or I will weep all over again.

After a leisurely breakfast on my balcony of veggie omelets, crisp and dry turkey bacon, and lattes with plenty of cinnamon, Asher announces he has something important to show me at his building.

"I think it will take up some time, so we should leave soon." He runs his fingers back and forth along his bottom lip, his thinking tell. "Let's bring Bisou and Jin along. I'll place my bags in the back of your car; we won't have time to come back here afterward."

"Are we going to the bookstore?" I question, very curious why this is so important.

"No." He stretches this short word out as if it might be enough of an answer and not garner any more questions.

"Okay. I'll prep the puppies. You go grab your bags."

Once we arrive at the building, we don't park on the street. Instead, Asher directs me around the corner to the secure tenant parking entrance. When we reach a big steel door, he pulls something out of his black backpack front pocket and hands it to me. A nondescript black keycard.

"This is yours to keep. The reader is sensitive, so all you need to do is be relatively close and hold up the card. No need to roll down your window."

I do as he instructs and the garage door slides open, closing behind me when my SUV is through. Asher doesn't direct me to any of the empty spots we come to. Instead, we come to another garage door, and I repeat the process from before.

Inside, is a small, clean parking lot of, maybe, a dozen spaces, but there is only one other car here and I recognize it as the Mercedes I rode in not too long ago. Gareth's Mercedes.

Asher points ahead. "You can park on the other side of the elevator, but all these spaces can be used by you with the exception of Gareth's space. Even with all the empty spaces available, I wouldn't be surprised if he has you towed if you park in his spot. I'm kidding, of course. At least, I think I am."

I giggle at his joking, relieved because he has been in no joking mood since Tuesday.

Bisou and Jin sniff like crazy at their new surroundings once out of my car. All I smell is newness. There has to be an air filtration system in this garage because it doesn't smell like any I've ever been in.

"As long as you have the keycard on your person, the elevator will be called down and open for you. This is a dedicated elevator to the penthouse level. You may enter and exit on this level, the ground floor, and level two, but the keycard you have is programmed differently. Only you, me, Gareth, and Ryan have access to this elevator."

The elevator dings its arrival, slides open, and we all step inside. Asher presses the penthouse button and as the door closes. I wonder why we are visiting Gareth today. I also wonder why I don't ask Asher. Instead, I look into one beveled mirrored wall and see Asher watching me, his expression expectant, but he asks nothing either.

When the elevator halts and the door opens, Asher allows the puppies and me off first. We step onto a green marble floor, an interesting color choice I contemplate for a few seconds until I look up and understand how the flooring blends into the lush greenery of a massive, glass-walled atrium.

I take a few steps to the middle of the hall, stop, and stare, stunned by the beauty before me. The atrium ceiling is much higher than the building's roof and pitched, and I can only imagine the kind of nighttime view of the stars it provides. There are well-maintained trees and bushes and flowerbeds, small grass areas with outdoor furniture perfect to get comfortable and read. In the center of it all is a swimming pool. Not Olympic-sized, but you could still do laps if you want.

This could be a luxury hotel!

"In order to access the atrium from here, you need to swipe your keycard against the reader. I didn't want the doors sliding open every time it sensed a card," Asher explains. "Gareth's apartment is to the left. Mine is to the right."

"Yours?" I peel my eyes from the atrium and turn to Asher.

"This is what I want you to see."

My head is swimming in confusion. All I can do is follow Asher through his front door.

After Asher shuts the front door, he bends down to unleash the puppies. "Jin has been here before. Bisou will be safe."

I nod as I look around the small foyer I'm standing in. I see the green marble floor ends here, opening up to a rich wood beyond this space. The ceiling and walls are a clean ivory. I register another door which I assume is a coat closet. There's a vintage round table in the center of the room with a beautiful marquetry inlay of roses in the center, around the perimeter, and down the four legs. I can picture a giant bouquet of bright pink roses on top of that table for a splash of color.

I feel a warm hand on my lower back, the gentle pressure urging me to move along. I allow Asher to guide me through his second home. Although, as we pass through a large living room full of new furniture and empty bookcases, this place has the feel of a model home never lived in. Each room Asher shows me is beautiful with a combination of restored antique and vintage wood furniture pieces mixed with new sofas in soft fabrics, leather armchairs, and area rugs. There are live plants and willowy trees staged in sun-drenched dead spaces, bringing the outdoors inside. Giant windows provide spectacular lake and city views. The well-appointed white kitchen looks into and has French door entry to the atrium, a small breakfast nook and counter seating, and glass-paned upper cabinet doors.

As we continue on, Asher points out two guest bedrooms, one of which has been turned into an office that has never been used judging by the lack of electronics here. We pass a laundry room and eventually come to open double doors at the end of the hallway; a large bedroom that can only be the owner's suite.

A massive, yet elegant, four-poster bed catches my eye first, hard not to. It faces a marble fireplace; the mantel reminds me of the one in November's library with the rose etchings. At the far window wall is a small sitting area with two comfortable armchairs, ottomans, and small vintage marble top table in between.

We move on to a huge bathroom with a huge clawfoot bathtub as the pièce de resistance. I barely notice the glass-walled shower behind, even though it has a skylight for the few plants on rock ledges inside to receive sunlight.

I cannot even fathom . . .

Asher begins to open the top drawers of the double-sink vanity for me to see the contents. "I bought duplicates of all your skincare and hair products. The hair dryer and other things you use. I'm sure I missed some things, so you might take a look. There are plenty of hangers in the closet and drawer space for your clothes. I also shopped for some groceries I placed in the pantry and refrigerator-"

"Why?" I cut Asher off from what I think is nervous rambling.

"Because I want you to stay here while I'm gone. I know you might have some very long workdays this week, and I would feel better if you didn't have to drive home after. After I adopted Jin, I had a dog run fence installed around one of the grass areas where she could be in the atrium and be safe. I want Jin and Bisou to have swim lessons in the pool, so they know how to get in and out safely."

"Asher, I don't understand. You have two apartments! Although the apartment next to mine is very nice, you have THIS!" I spread my arms wide, then drop them to my sides. "Help me understand."

Asher stares, gathers his thoughts. I expect a long answer to come forth, but all he says is, "You don't live here."

I step close, place the palms of my hands on his chest. "This building is not far from the other."

"Before we started sleeping in the same bed together, I liked knowing you were on the other side of the wall. I was going to move here. I was planning to start packing up not long after you moved in. Then I got to know you and thought if I moved, maybe we wouldn't see each other, but I had to know you. I wanted you to know me, so I stayed and fell in love and now, I don't want to live here without you." He takes a much-needed breath before continuing. "I know we haven't been together long, but I do know you are it for me. So, at some point in time, until you feel the same, I'm staying where I am. I don't want to live here without you."

I take another look around this beautiful sanctuary of a bathroom. It's been created to share with one other person. Whether Asher knows it or not, he manifested me or a love like this or whatever. This place he carefully planned and built is magnificent, and to not live in it makes my heart crack.

I've barely lived in my apartment two months, barely known Asher that long. Regardless, Asher is making it known that I am the woman he wants to spend his life with. He's so confident in speaking his intention; zero hesitation. Should I feel nervous? I'm not. Asher feels right to me too. I can't envision my life without him. But practically, I have ten months remaining on my lease.

Jin and Bisou wander inside the bedroom after their exploring, find us and look like they're wondering what's next. Should they be ready to leave? Should they find a soft spot to hunker down for a nap here? I'm not really sure myself.

"Genevieve, you don't have to stay here if you don't want to, but please know I will feel better knowing you are safe and not driving home each night exhausted. Ultimately, it's your decision."

"You're right. I'll pick up some clothes and supplies for the dogs after dropping you off at the airport."

"Everything you need for the kids is here: food, treats,

and bowls in the kitchen; toys in a basket in the living room; beds in the bedroom and living room."

I step into him, wrap my arms around his waist and rest my head under his chin. "When did you have time to get this all done?"

"When it's important, I make time." He holds me, placing a lingering kiss to the crown of my head. "It's time to go."

"One more minute," I say around a lump in my throat.

He gathers me closer, tighter. "One more minute."

I breathe him in, and he does the same of me.

Asher

Asher, who usually attends client meetings with Rhys, was excused from future meetings during this trip because Rhys said, "I can feel annoyance emitting from you. Go do something." Asher and Rhys split up tasks where they can to get the job done faster, because regardless of what Rhys says, he wants to get back home as soon as possible too.

The problem with working alone: too much time to think.

Asher dwells on how he's disappointing Genevieve, even though she assures him he isn't. He ponders how he could be helping her right now. He remembers how she feels . . .

He misses Genevieve so much; it hurts to breathe.

Chapter Twenty-Six

Sleep did not come easily last night. The penthouse apartment is too new. The bed is comfortable but doesn't smell like Asher. Nothing here does. I know that's why Jin kept rising from her doggy bed: to roam the apartment in search of her dad. She was fine all day, but it's the middle of the night now and he's not where he's supposed to be.

None of us are.

I do the thing I never do because Bisou and Jin are small dogs and beds are high; I would never want them to get hurt jumping off. Yet, after the third time of Asher's daughter looking for her one true love, I scoop up both puppies and hold them close. At dawn, I drive to Asher's apartment . . . current apartment . . . old apartment–whatever–and grab our pillows from his bed and dig four of his T-shirts from the laundry hamper. When I return to the penthouse, I place the pillows on the bed, then line each dog bed in the bedroom with a T-shirt. The remaining two I take downstairs to their puppy pen in the bookstore.

Luckily for me, November is an early riser and arrives at

the store at seven, ready to get to work. Astrid taught me how to use the espresso machine properly, and I am able to make myself and my best friend whole milk lattes with freshly ground cinnamon; an extra shot of espresso for me.

"When I talked to Rhys last night, he said dinner with Asher was a short one; Asher just wanted to go back to his hotel room. Rhys said he will be rewording future contracts and remove this beck and call clause." She pauses for a sip from her cup but changes her mind when she feels it might be too hot. "It was fine pre-the-women-in-their-lives entered the picture, but life is different for the men now. More planning should be involved. Rhys feels bad for Asher, and a bit for himself, because Rhys thought it would be fun to do something different and help me here at the store this week."

"Please tell Rhys, as I told Asher, none of this is their fault. I have you here and staff and we're all committed to getting the store looking all sparkly for opening. It's good to hear that Rhys' outlook on life has changed because of you, but this week, we will be fine. What could possibly go wrong?"

I had to ask. Famous. Last. Words.

The first thing to go wrong is an employee not showing up for work today. No messages from Rebecca. When I call, she "decided to go with another job."

"Considering you were hired here and today is Orientation, you didn't think it would be a good idea to let me know?"

"That's today?" Rebecca sounds completely baffled.

I should have known when I didn't receive responses to my emails.

I share this with Asher when we talk at night, my eleven p.m. to his eight p.m., me lying in bed, him back at work after having dinner with Rhys. I don't share the computer system glitch temporarily wiping out inventory. A nice man named Teddy from tech services was able to solve that problem and stave off my panic. Asher would feel terrible that he couldn't help, and he doesn't need to feel worse than he already does for not being here.

"I'm short staffed now, but I'd rather that than have an unreliable employee later on," I share.

I have the puppies on the bed and my cell phone on speaker, so Jin can hear her daddy. She knows it's him because she goes from cocking her head side to side, to wagging her tail when he says her name or other key words. My heart snags when I see Jin rest her head between her paws, nose touching the edge of the phone, and she looks so defeated. Another thing I don't share with Asher.

"What are you going to do?" I hear what sounds like metal clanking against metal in whatever he is assembling.

"November and Astrid offered to handle a second interview with two good candidates off the list I saved while I continue training the employees that did show up. I wish more kids from Perseverance were interested in romance books. Lucy is great, learning quickly, and taking notes." I scratch the top of Jin's head the way she likes, but it doesn't shift her mood. "Astrid told me the two young men she's training as baristas are stellar. In my opinion, they're hanging on her every word because they both have mad crushes."

"Typical." Asher chuckles. "I do know that feeling of wanting to do everything right under the eyes of your crush. Fortunate for me, my crush became the love of my life."

"Lucky for me too."

Tuesday's problem: November, Astrid, and I arrive to frigid air in the bookstore. Immediately, I call Ryan and he has someone come over to work the problem, but none of the employees, all dressed for warm weather, are able to stand the cold for more than thirty minutes and I don't want them too. Astrid pivots and goes to a local farmer's market to pick up a few ingredients to teach her staff to make fresh tisanes. Instead of sending the rest of the staff home, I send them to the French café around the corner and tell them to order what they want on me. November and I take this opportunity to sneak away to Asher's penthouse.

"Holy. Shit." The two words spill from November's mouth. She stands exactly where I stood two days ago, facing the atrium.

"Yeah."

When I open the front door to Asher's apartment, November hesitates walking in. Instead, she starts walking backward toward the elevator.

"Hold the door open for me," she says, giant evil grin plastered on her pretty face, and I know exactly what she's about to do.

She turns and jogs to Gareth's front door, then rings and rings and rings his doorbell before hauling ass back to me. I close the door behind her, and we both stay quiet and listen. Bisou and Jin look at us, tails wagging, probably trying to figure out the game we're playing and how they can join in the fun.

I'm pretty sure Gareth is home if his car in the parking garage is any indication. I'm right, because we hear his door open, then the stepping sound of dress shoes halfway down the hall. I picture him looking through the atrium doors before turning around and returning to his apartment. When we hear the door close, we laugh until we can't breathe.

As much fun as that was, it takes nearly three hours for the air conditioning problem to resolve, setting the schedule behind. It wouldn't be that big of a deal, but I receive a phone call from a very nice lady in Buffalo, Minnesota, stating she received several boxes of mine on her front porch. Eight boxes of books I was expecting to arrive this morning. It takes another couple of hours on the phone with customer service to get the issue resolved, but when we hang up, I'm not quite sure the replacement shipment will arrive by Saturday. If not, the YA section will be a little light at the grand opening.

I wasn't going to tell Asher any of it, but, of course, Ryan would need to notify Asher of an electrical snafu like this. When Asher calls me midday, he sounds tired and frazzled as he explains what went wrong with the temperature sensors, and he's pretty sure it won't happen again.

"Asher, you don't need to be bothering with this." I speak carefully, softly. "The problem has been fixed, and you have your own work to focus on."

He blows out a breath. "If I were there, the problem might have been fixed sooner. I know this glitch set you back-"

I hear the tightness of stress in his voice and have to make it stop. "I love you for caring so much, but, really, I'm fine. Problems solved."

"Problems? Plural?" Asher misses nothing.

I'm not about to lie, but at least I can gloss over it.

If I thought yesterday's problems were something to write home about, turns out they are a pinprick in comparison to today's knife in the gut.

My day begins with me behind the cashier counter, standing on a ladder, staging faux bougainvillea up the side of the white breakfront and along the top, made to look like it's climbing up toward the ceiling. Since summer is nearly here, I thought to create a display of travel romances here for an impulse buy grab. The bougainvillea is a great complement and splash of color.

There's a knock on the front door and I see Gareth through the window. I climb down the ladder, cross the entry, and unlock the door for him.

"Hey! What brings you here?" I ask as he steps inside.

"I think you owe me a cup of coffee for your little prank. I think a cappuccino to go sounds good to me."

My eyes narrow at him; my hands go to my hips.

"Didn't Asher tell you about the cameras in the hallway?" His smirk is vile, but he has me there.

"You win. Cappuccino to go it is. Follow me."

We pass through the seating area of the coffee bar where I have the puppies stashed for the day. With all the employees wandering around, I don't want them underfoot. I do see someone left two stacks of boxes here when I told them all to keep the coffee bar clean and clear. I'm trying to contain the merchandise mess to the bookstore side.

"Well, hello, little ones!" Gareth stops, leans over one side of the puppy pen and greets Jin and Bisou who are wiggling and licking their hellos.

"I see a doggie in Uncle Gareth's future, don't you?" I baby talk to the puppies and take their extra wiggles as agreement.

"No, no. That's absolutely out of the question." He gives them a last pet, then straightens to his full height and glances at the coffee bar. "I see Astrid's here. I can bother her for coffee and leave you to your work."

I look to see Astrid, standing tall behind the bar, arms folded across her chest, glaring at Gareth. It feels very *Sundown at the O.K. Corral* and I'm not sure I should leave the two of them alone. I take a couple steps forward, then remember I didn't lock the front door.

Gareth's eyes are on Astrid. He's following too close and doesn't see me turn around. Like dominoes, one tips over and they all fall, and it happens too fast for me to do anything about it. I collide with Gareth's chest, and he topples back, reactively reaching for the boxes to keep himself upright. He does stay standing, but the top boxes tip over into the puppy pen.

A clear, high-pitch cry emits from under the boxes.

"No!" I scream, and scramble to get to the puppies. I don't see that Gareth is right there with me. I don't see where I'm throwing boxes. I don't see November and Astrid and others running to help. It's like everything on the peripheral is hazy.

Gareth gets to Bisou first and picks her up, but she's not the one crying. Jin is trapped under a box. I gauge the weight as I swiftly pick it up and toss it; it's not heavy as far as I can tell in my state, but Jin is shaking and whimpering and can't seem to stand.

"It's okay, Jin." I speak in the softest tones, my vision going blurry with tears. "It's okay, baby."

I reach into the pen and lightly stroke her fur to assess where she might be hurt and how I'm going to pick her up. She cries out when I touch her back leg and I jerk my hand away.

Tears begin to streak my cheeks. "I need to get Jin to the vet."

"I'll drive!" November shouts.

"No! I'll drive," Gareth commands, and he is no longer the jokester. "November, you continue here. You know what you're doing, and I wouldn't be much help in the store. I'll drive."

Even if I cared to argue, I couldn't because he's right.

"Don't worry about the bookstore," November begins.

"Consider everything handled here," Astrid ends.

I grab both of Asher's T-shirts in the corner of the pen, then gently wrap Jin in them. She has stopped crying, but trembles, terrified by everything and everyone in this moment. I take a deep breath before easing my hands under her small body and lifting as carefully as possible into my arms. She whimpers and more of my tears fall.

"Let's go." I look to Gareth and it's the first I'm really seeing Bisou. She shakes in his arms as he strokes her fur. I want to reach out to my sweet girl, but I'm afraid to remove my arms from their position around Jin. I feel like I have failed both of them.

Gareth leads the way to his sedan parked on the street, probably because he was on his way to work. He opens the passenger side door for me, and I carefully situate myself in the seat, click the seatbelt, then retrieve my cell phone from the thigh pocket of my leggings. I rest Jin on my left thigh and cradle her in my left arm. When I'm ready for her, Gareth places Bisou on my right thigh, then carefully shuts my door. Bisou immediately glues her little body into mine and I want to cry all over again. I press my lips to the top of her head as I scroll through my phone.

When Gareth slides into the driver's seat and buckles up, I hand him my phone.

"Here are the directions to the animal emergency my vet recommended."

He syncs my phone to his car's Bluetooth, and we are on the way.

"I should call Asher." I hear the tremble in my voice.

"Terrible idea." His hands grip the steering wheel almost imperceptibly tighter. "There's nothing he can do from three thousand miles away, and you shouldn't call him until you have all the facts."

I nod and look down at the puppies on my lap and think how Asher held them in his like this when we brought them home that first day. My reminiscing is interrupted by Gareth's voice.

"I'm sorry about what happened."

"This was an accident." I look up to him, but he won't even glance my way. "No one is to blame."

"Still. I'm sorry."

I do wait to call Asher when I have all the facts. The X-rays showed no signs of a break or fracture. There is some swelling that the vet said is normal for a severe contusion of this kind, and Jin will need to be babied for a few weeks. Only short, leashed walks. No roughhousing with Bisou, of course. Bisou seems to comprehend her sister is not well and has been very careful with her. I did have Bisou checked out and, thankfully, she is fine.

Once I'm back at the penthouse and have the puppies settled on the living room sofa, I text Asher to see if he's free for a video chat. I want him to see Jin is okay when I tell him. Yes, I am grateful I didn't call him right away. I'm calmer now that I have all the information. If I had called Asher on the way to the hospital, I probably would have been bawling my eyes out and saying something stupid like, "I broke your puppy."

Although, after splashing water on my face a little while ago, Asher will know I've been crying; my eyes are still red rimmed and puffy, and I can't find eye drops.

Asher's video chat rings through and I answer before the first ring ends.

"Hey!" I try to sound cheerful, but my voice isn't conveying that.

His eyebrows immediately furrow. "What's wrong?"

God, he sounds stressed.

Jin's ears perk up at hearing her daddy's voice and I turn the camera lens to his puppy.

"Is Jin wrapped in my T-shirts?"

"I thought they would comfort her." I don't dare say that I had them here from day one because Jin was feeling glum. Instead, I spill the contents of the morning, and what the vet said.

"I am so sorry, Asher. You entrusted me with Jin and I fucked up. I know it was an accident, but still. I am so sorry."

Asher stares at Jin for many seconds. He removes his eyeglasses from his nose and rubs his eyes before returning the glasses. Watching him hold back tears guts me.

"It was an accident, Genevieve. I'm sure this isn't the only time something will happen to one of the puppies. How is Bisou?"

"Shaken up. Exhausted. But she's fine."

"Good. I'm sorry you had to deal with this, Love. Please keep me posted if anything . . ."

"I will. I'm staying with Jin and Bisou in the penthouse for the remainder of the day. I have work I can do on my laptop, and November said she will video chat with me in an hour, so I can see the progress, give instructions, etcetera."

"Thank you." He runs his free hand through his longish locks. "I'm so sorry I'm not there."

"Please don't do that to yourself. This is beyond your control. Beyond mine. Beyond anyone's."

None of this is sitting well with him, regardless of what I say.

Asher gazes into my eyes through the screen. "I love you so much."

I gaze right back. "I love you more."
He disconnects the call, but I keep staring at my phone.

Asher

All Asher can think is: I need to go home!

Chapter Twenty-Seven
GENEVIEVE

It takes a village.

In a space where the coffee bar meets the bookstore, November and I stand side by side, taking in the beauty of it all. Shelves are stocked. (No, the YA books didn't arrive, but November made do with adding an assortment of candles and other merchandise to the empty spaces.) Decor is perfectly staged. All is clean and welcoming.

"I've never felt the saying 'a dream come true' until this moment," I say just above a whisper.

November slings an arm around my shoulders and squeezes. "You did good."

"We all did good. I couldn't have gotten through this week without you and everyone else. Even Alex and Carys pitched in when I couldn't be here on Wednesday. Thank you for calling them, by the way. I'm going to have to deliver a big basket of the Warm Heart tea to Alex and you can tell me what from here Carys will like."

"I'll tell you right now. Carys will be totally into all the fun skincare products and a selection of fuzzy socks."

"Done. And you may take whatever you want for your-self and lifetime free coffee drinks."

"Just the free coffee will do. Anything more will feel like armed robbery."

After shutting down the coffee bar for the night, Astrid comes to join us. "It looks amazing. Five stars. Wish I could give more."

The rest of the employees were sent home three hours ago to be bright-eyed and bushy-tailed for the big day tomorrow.

"Do you need anything else from me, Boss Lady?" Astrid asks.

"Go home and rest," I reply. "You have to be here early in the morning."

"Then I bid you both, good night." Astrid hoists her tote higher on her shoulder.

"See you tomorrow," November says. She's tired but still manages to push up the corners of her mouth into a smile.

"Thank you for all your hard work, Astrid," I say, because I feel she genuinely needs to be acknowledged. "What you turned the coffee bar into is far better than I could have done myself."

"Thank you. It's been fun." With that, Astrid saunters out and locks the door behind her.

I turn to November. "There's nothing left for you to do but go home, take a shower, and sleep."

"Are you sure? I can stay. Do you need help getting the dogs upstairs?"

"We'll be fine. I'm going to take one last look around while I turn off all the lights, then head upstairs."

"I know you won't be sleeping tonight but try to get some rest."

She knows me so well.

I walk November to the door and give her a tight hug.

"Remember, parking is going to be insane tomorrow, so I'll buzz you in to park underground."

"Got it." She gives me one more hug before exiting into the light of the setting sun. I lock the door behind her.

While the lights are still on, I check how I look in the leaning mirror close to the cashier counter. I have pretty mirrors all over the store, like the large ones hanging on the red brick wall behind the coffee bar. Not only are they aesthetically pleasing, but useful to see what's going on all over the store.

I fix my hair, pinch my cheeks, then pull a tube of Strawberry Lip Smacker from the front pocket of my denim cutoffs and give my lips a tidy swipe. I still look like I slept a dozen hours over the last five days, but I don't care; I want to make one more post to all the social media accounts to hype Mine's grand opening. The follower count has grown exponentially; I'm not sure what to expect from attendance tomorrow.

After I finish posting, just as I'm about to take one final stroll through the store, there's a knock at the front door. The pups rouse from their sound sleep on their cushy beds by Asher and my table.

The front window shades are rolled down for the night, so no one can see inside. My cell phone chimes in my back pocket. I pull out my phone and see Asher sent me a text.

> I'm at the front door. Please, please let
> me in.

I sprint to the door. Bisou and Jin sit up as I pass, alert by my commotion. With shaking hands, I fumble with the lock and fling the door open.

Asher is all rumpled clothing, disheveled hair, dark circles, kaleidoscope eyes a little unfocused behind his Clark Kent-style eyeglasses, even as they zero in on me.

He is the most beautiful thing I have ever seen.

"Hi," Asher croaks out as if really thirsty.

I leap into his arms, wrapping all my limbs around him tight. A sob escapes my lips in harmony with the puppies' happy whimpers; their daddy is home!

My love is HOME!!!

Asher envelopes me in his arms, buries his face into my neck and inhales deep.

"I'm home," he whispers.

I know he's not talking about a place; he's talking about *me*.

"How are you here?" Disbelief is plainly heard in my wobbly voice. "You still have a few days on your project."

Asher sets me back on the ground, wheels his luggage inside, and I lock the door after him.

He parks his suitcases and drops his backpack. Bisou and the limping Jin are going bonkers for their dad's attention.

He bends down to scoop Jin up, careful of her hind leg. "Oh, my sweet girl, how are you?" Jin rubs her head all over Asher's face. "Yes, Jin. I know. I missed you too."

Tears well in my eyes from sheer relief that Jin is reunited with Asher. Asher is home and everything feels right in the world. I pick up Bisou and hug her, but she only has heart eyes for Asher. I don't blame her; we all do. He gives Bisou the scratches behind the ears she's waiting for, then he cups my jaw with his hand, swiping away a rogue tear with his thumb.

"I had to be here for the grand opening. Be here for you. I pulled a few all-nighters to get the job done, but I knew I had to be on a plane today. Rhys stayed behind for one last client meeting and will fly home tomorrow."

My heart sails over Asher standing right here. I shift Bisou to my right arm and plant my left hand on Asher's bicep, push up on my sneakered toes, and tilt my head back for a kiss. Asher obliges by brushing his lips lightly against mine before pressing in fully.

"I missed you so fucking much," Asher whispers against my lips before deepening the kiss.

The kiss is short-lived because the puppies begin wiggling between us for attention, their whines pitiful.

Asher and I laugh. And it's the happiest sound I've heard in what feels like forever.

We gather Asher's things and head toward the back of the store to exit, turning off the lights along the way. The last book section we pass is the dark romance corner and it's gorgeous with black, almost Gothic-style bookshelves. November outdid herself with the hot pink faux roses staged along the top and cascading halfway down each endcap. The two hot pink velvet armchairs with a claw-foot side table on a black area rug is dramatic and stunning.

Jin has finally calmed in her daddy's arms, sleepy-eyed and resting her head under his chin. I think it's going to be a long, long time until she lets him out of her sight again.

"Are you sure there isn't anything left to do?" Asher asks, as we shuffle down the hall toward the elevator.

"The only things I want to do is shower together and fall asleep in your arms."

The elevator door slides open and we step inside. I press the penthouse button.

"Showering and sleeping with you sounds like a solid plan for me too, Love."

Love.

When I hear the nickname, the only one he uses, it strikes me that it's not just a nickname. I am the entirety of his love. His only family. His person.

I plan on earning that nickname every day, never taking it for granted. Just as I know Asher will never take my love for him for granted. He values it highly as something so precious and priceless because he's never had it. I want to see love through his lens.

Oh, what I have learned about love these last two months!

Later, surprising to me or perhaps not surprising at all, in bed with Asher wrapped around me, I sleep soundly through the night until my alarm wakes me at six a.m. on Grand Opening Day.

Dream to reality.

Asher

Every single one of Asher's days that Genevieve is a part of is something to revel in.

Today?

He gets to witness a monumental one.

Chapter Twenty-Eight

First thing this morning, after the alarm clock on my cell phone sounds off, Asher and I decide the game plan for the day is Asher will stay in the penthouse with the puppies. I have no idea what the headcount will be today, but I do know it will be a lot, too much for the kids, especially Jin who is nursing her injured hind leg.

I know Asher would like to clone himself and be in both places at the same time, but it's not feasible for him to hang around the store for hours at a time. He won't be missing all of today. I am truly grateful for this penthouse apartment because Asher will come down for the ribbon cutting at ten o'clock, then stop by throughout the day to check in. If the crowd thins out, he'll bring his camera and the puppies on leashes to take some opening day pictures with me.

Speaking of pictures, I narrow down my outfit choices to two that I believe will photograph well. I hired a professional photographer for the morning to capture as much of this important day as possible. I stand to the side of the bed and hold up two halter dresses for Asher to view; I want to show off my butterfly tattoo today since it is the logo of my store.

Asher lays in bed, Jin curled in a ball over his heart and takes his time assessing the options. "I love you in both dresses but save the yellow for another time. With all the activity today, it might be too long a length to deal with."

"Rose pink it is then." I step forward and give him a quick kiss before returning the yellow dress to the walk-in closet.

"Would you like me to make you something for breakfast?" he asks.

"No, thank you. November is picking up breakfast sandwiches I pre-ordered, and Astrid is making coffee for our staff meeting." On my way to the bathroom, I point toward his chest. "Besides, I don't think Jin is going to allow you to move."

Thirty minutes later, I'm dressed and primped and ready to dive into this soon-to-be whirlwind of a day. I look at my reflection in the large mirror over the vanity, and my heart begins to race. Everything in my life is coming up roses. I feel like crying happy tears. Although I'm wearing waterproof mascara, the last thing I need is to look red-eyed and blotchy.

"November's here!" Asher calls out to me. "I buzzed her in!"

I step out of the bathroom and give Asher a twirl in my dress.

"You're stunning. Always so beautiful." His throat works and I can see his Adam's apple bob. "I need to kiss you."

He begins to sit up to Jin's dismay, and I quickly step forward.

"Stay there. Let Jin have her time with you; she's been through it."

He snakes an arm around my waist as I lean forward to kiss his lips, and it's exactly what I need to ground me before the craziness of the day begins.

After our breakfast meeting, and everyone has their assignments, the vendors I hired for today's event begin to arrive and set up. Astrid's adoring crew already set up their pop-up tent and logo clothed tables for the free coffee drinks to be served to customers waiting in line. The pink cupcake truck parks at the curb, ready to pass out four hundred free-bies in a few flavors personally chosen by moi. The female tattoo artist I'm collaborating with today sets up shop in a velvet-roped-off corner of the coffee bar and tells me she's excited to be completely pre-booked for the bookish flash tattoos on offer. I also have Nadia, the candlemaker, here setting up a table with extra stock because I know the candles will fly out the door.

Lucy and Lucas, who is far more versed in sports romance than I will ever be, will stay behind the cashier counter. Naturally sunny dispositioned and die-hard dark romance fan Yvette is my door person, making sure there aren't too many people in the store at once, to talk books with the customers in line, and collect raffle tickets for the gift card prizes.

November has been placed in charge of coordinating the author book signings, also located in the coffee bar's seating section. And I will be wherever I am needed most. To keep things flowing, I decided to rope off the coffee bar, keeping it closed to purchases. Astrid will be stationed there to prepare the fresh beverages to be given away. Even though Alex will be by soon to volunteer a few hours before she has to leave for her daughter, Plum's, soccer game, I would have loved an additional employee here, but I'll make do.

I receive a text from Asher asking me to let Gareth in the back entrance to pick up a couple cappuccinos. I place the order with Astrid, then walk to the back of the store to open the door.

Inside, Gareth takes a good look around as we walk to the coffee bar.

"Well done, Gen. You have the magic touch. This bookstore. Asher. Asher is a completely different person. In a good way."

I'm moved because Gareth is being sincere with his words.

"That's kind of you to say."

"Did Asher tell you I will be hanging out with him upstairs today? Whenever he wants to come down here, I will keep an eye on the dogs. It's the least I can do for breaking his."

"Stop feeling so responsible. But I appreciate you."

"Do you need me to stay? Help out around here?"

I give Gareth a quick once over. "Probably a good idea for you not to stick around. The customers might think you're a book cover model and want pictures with you."

"That might be a good time." Of course he grins.

"Go get your coffee, Gareth, and go back upstairs."

We part ways and I hear him laugh out loud.

I glance at the cell phone in my hand. Thirty minutes until ribbon cutting. I text Asher.

Coffee is on its way!

Do you need anything? I can come down and help.

> Everything's going smoothly, knock on
> wood. See you soon.

I love you!

I love you more!

November sidles up to me as I slip my phone back into one of my dress pockets-*love dresses with pockets*-but before November can open her mouth to speak, we hear an interesting conversation coming from the coffee bar. We stay absolutely still and listen.

"Okay, Gary."

"Do not bastardize my name," scolds Gareth. "How would you feel if I called you, Ass?"

"I think that name better suits you," Astrid retorts.

"I may be an asshole, but I am no ass, Sassy Pants." Gareth picks up the to-go cups that Astrid places on the bar between them.

Astrid's eyes narrow. "Keep telling yourself that, Pretty Boy."

"At least you think I'm pretty."

Before Astrid can get in another word, Gareth turns away from the pick-up counter and passes me and November on his way out without noticing our nonverbal freak out of a conversation.

'Did you hear that???' I convey.

'What's going on with that???' She eyeballs back.

We see Lucy fast approaching, and we say at the same time, "Later."

"Have you seen outside?" Lucy is absolutely giddy, bouncing on the balls of her sneakered feet.

When I don't respond right away, Lucy grabs hold of

my hand and leads me to the front door, November following close behind.

My eyes take a few seconds to adjust to the morning sunlight, but I smell freshly-cut grass on a breeze, brewing coffee, and mouth-watering buttercream. And I hear a whole lot of chatter and closest to me, November's voice as she sucks in her breath.

"Oh. My. God."

I look right, the direction November and Lucy are staring.

People, no, customers, line the sidewalk all the way to the corner.

November takes out her cell phone and starts shooting video as we walk, and I'm glad she's capturing this, because when we get to the end it doesn't stop there. More customers sip signature coffee drinks and munch on cupcakes around the corner too, and around the next. Some wave to me, probably recognizing me from my social media posts.

Hundreds of people wait in line to help celebrate my shop.

Blotchiness be damned–tears spill over my waterproof mascara-clad bottom lashes.

We close Mine at the pre-scheduled four p.m. today; I knew the staff would be here earlier than usual, the excitement would be draining, and I want them well-rested before another anticipated bustling day.

We did a decent job restocking the shelves throughout the day, but everyone has their assignment for the remaining hour on the clock after close. Astrid and her coffee bar crew pull the outdoor equipment inside, clean, take quick inventory, and, finally, reset the bar for the morning. I walk every inch of the store with a garbage bag and gloved hands, seeking any coffee cups or other trash left behind, and straightening any displays gone askew.

Lucy restocks gift items. Lucas and Yvette restock books. Lucas gazes longingly at Lucy every time she's in close proximity, or afar, and Lucy hasn't a clue. I have to smile at the potential of love blooming under the roof of a romance only bookstore, if Lucas can get Lucy to even notice him beyond coworker status.

James and Ryan stopped by to wish me well. Both excited for me over the constant crowd of customers which was nice to hear, but I couldn't help feeling the connection between the two. When Ryan went to pick up coffee for the two of them, I had to ask James if they were a thing.

"Oh, no!" James exclaimed, waving me off with her hand. "We're just old friends. We went to high school together once upon a time ago."

The lady doth protest too much, methinks.

Say what she will, I didn't miss the blush bloom on her cheeks before she walked away to join Ryan.

My attention is drawn to the appearance of two black and white furry wiggle worms at my feet and the man I love with my whole heart holding their leashes. I remove my gloves and toss them into the garbage bag before placing the bag on the floor in front of a Friends-to-Lovers display.

Two seconds later, my arms are wrapped tight around Asher's waist as his free arm wraps around mine. I rest my chin against his sternum and look up. He places a sweet kiss on my forehead and looks down at my face.

"Thank you," I say.

"For the kiss?"

"If it hadn't been for you, this shop wouldn't exist today."

"Love, I can't take credit for that. This is all you."

I shake my head. "You provided me with the place when I couldn't find one. You pushed the remodel along so I could have this day. I take complete credit for my ideas, my drive, and how this all turned out in the end, but if it weren't for you . . ." I sigh. "My love, none of this would have begun."

Asher stays quiet, his hazel eyes even more stunning behind his eyeglasses because they are brimming with elation. With love.

"Then I need to thank you," he speaks softly.

"For what?"

"If you hadn't extended your friendship to me . . ." His voice cracks, but he takes a breath before continuing on. "I might never have known love."

Cup after cup after cup, my heart is overflowing.

Gushing.

Epilogue

Asher

I push up the sleeves of my navy cotton sweater, and my eyes catch on the small tattoo along my inner forearm. The tips of my fingers run over the souvenir from the grand opening of my love's bookstore. During the event that day, as a surprise I pre-booked for her, I had Genevieve sit on my lap and handwrite 'Love you' on this patch of my skin for the tattoo artist to trace over. She surprised me back by having me sign my first name on the back of her right shoulder. When I asked if she was sure, Genevieve responded, "You could never be a regret."

From where I sit at the cool marble table Genevieve has reserved only for our use, my eyes seek out the object of all my affection. Well, maybe a little of that affection goes to our puppies. I spot her walking a customer to the cashier counter, animatedly talking with her hands undoubtedly about the books in the customer's hands.

My love looks like December perfection in a cream-colored sweater dress that hits mid-thigh, caramel leather belt cinching her hourglass waist, and matching over-the-knee boots with short, stacked heels. Her soft, long curls cascade down her back. My hands itch to touch her, to wrap myself around her to keep her warm. Genevieve hasn't adjusted to cold temperatures yet. Fortunately, her commute to work doesn't require her to step outside if she doesn't want to.

During the summer, I met all of Genevieve's brothers as each made the trek to check out her thriving bookstore. Maman, as Genevieve's mother asked me to call her, stayed the entire month of October with us in the penthouse. Maman doted on her grandpuppies, worked in the bookstore with her daughter, and spent a significant amount of time getting to know me. After Halloween, Maman returned to her home in Paris, and Genevieve made the decision to move into the penthouse permanently.

We spent the weeks before Thanksgiving packing up our apartments and moving everything into our new home together. Her navy velvet sofa has replaced the armchairs in our bedroom, and we can be found reading there at night before bedtime. Yes, I'm still reading from her collection of romance novels. I've read everything by Ali Hazelwood, Kennedy Ryan, Emily Henry, Abby Jimenez, Tarah DeWitt, and started branching out to romantasy.

November and Rhys hosted Thanksgiving dinner this year, and the holiday felt so different for me than previous years. If I was invited somewhere. I went. If I wasn't, it was just another day on the calendar. This time, I sat beside the love of my life; the holiday meant something more to me and I was truly thankful. The next day, Genevieve and I went Christmas tree shopping and loaded several trees into the back of my truck, a few for the penthouse and a few for the bookstore. How beautiful she looked in her excitement to celebrate our first Christmas together with our dogs in our new home. It's contagious, and I'm full of the holiday spirit.

My Christmas shopping for Genevieve is done, well, at least her big present; I have other things to buy to make sure she feels completely spoiled. While Maman was in town, I asked if we could visit her in Paris during cherry blossom season. I also asked Maman for permission to marry Genevieve, swearing on my life, to forever take of her daughter. Maman's eyes swelled with tears, and she hugged me so tight as she gave me her blessing.

"It is crystal clear the love you have for each other. This is real. I could not have asked for a better man for my only daughter."

Every time I remember her words, my chest warms. You have no idea how scared I was that she might tell me, "No." Or tell me I'm not good enough. Sometimes those inadequate feelings creep up, and I have to remind myself that I am not that person anymore.

November helped me shop for a blue diamond engagement ring, blue because of the butterflies Genevieve loves so much. Maman took the ring back to Paris with her for safekeeping, and so Genevieve won't discover it at home.

This morning, as I sip my cinnamon latte, Genevieve thinks I'm finishing up a project. I am, just not for work. I finished booking our trip to Paris including a Seine River cruise where at some place that feels right, I will propose. If I can wait that long.

I feel the familiar pressure of two front paws against my knee; Jin wanting my attention. I shut my laptop closed and pick her up, as she requires, and place her on my lap.

"Hello, my sweet girl. Did you have a good nap, my sleepy daughter?"

Her hind leg completely healed, and I have been completely forgiven by Jin for that horrible time in her life, by the way. She stands on it along with the other, placing her front paws against my chest. She looks at me and makes a movement with her head that seems like she's saying 'yes.' My cheeks pull tight as I grin and I'm slowly becoming acquainted with this sensation on the regular. *Happiness.*

"I've been waiting for you to stop working." Genevieve slides into the only other chair at the table. Her chair.

"Do you need me for something?" I ask.

Genevieve glances down at Bisou stretching on her side in her bed before falling back to sleep. "I-"

She's looking over my shoulder now, beyond the windowpane, and looks completely dazzled by something.

"Oh!" That's all she speaks before rising from her chair and hurries out the front door without her coat.

I set Jin in her bed, tell her to stay, and follow Genevieve out where I find her standing on the sidewalk, arms stretched out in front of her, reaching for . . . snowflakes.

Big, fat, fluffy snowflakes drifting along, guided by gravity in their gentle descent.

Genevieve has never seen snowfall before. The enchantment in her glistening eyes, her rosy parted lips, is something to behold. She is always something to behold.

I can't help myself; I gather my whole world in my arms as she giggles in delight. Snowflakes settle in her curls, reminding me of the cherry blossoms that once landed there. Her cheeks and nose are already turning pink from the cold air, and all the love she has for me shimmers in her golden-brown eyes.

Without question, I know Genevieve can see that same abundance of love reflected back at her. She probably has it memorized because it's always there.

It always will be.

Author Ramblings

When I introduced Asher Adams in *Falling*, I knew I had to crack open his chest and take a look inside. What I found was a broken boy who has done well in taking care of himself, all on his own, but that's all he feels he's allowed to have. Love has never been an option.

Falling was written in dual POV because I knew it would be interesting to know what was going on in both November's and Rhys' minds and, boy, was that fun to write. When it was time to write *Mine*, I knew I would change the POV to first person because I wanted my readers to discover the bits and pieces of Asher as Genevieve does.

I know many readers thought/hoped Genevieve would end up with Gareth (his story is next in the series), but I knew Genevieve was the perfect catalyst for Asher's growth and no one would be able to give Genevieve the all-consuming love she clearly deserves like Asher can. I am deeply in love with the way these two are with each other. I also felt protective of Asher which made this book difficult for me to write without a box of tissues nearby, many breaks from my laptop, and lots of snacks to emotionally eat.

Because of my issues with writing *Mine*, I have to give a shout out to my editor Sam Stringert. Thank you, Sam, for being so patient and forgiving of my deadline changes. Thank you for your hard work of whipping *Mine* into shape!

I didn't have a playlist for *Falling* because it wasn't important for November and Rhys. I don't think I even listened to much music while writing *Falling*, probably because I was too busy listening to the dual narration of my MC's in my head. In *Mine*, though, I thought about the multitude of ways people utilize music including working through strong emotions. It's this reason I thought Asher would listen to certain songs to work through his thoughts and feelings and to feel less alone. Music is his constant companion. I painstakingly selected the songs in *Mine* for too many reasons to list, but the main reason is who Asher is. Yes, there are songs Genevieve listens to and I picked those for different reasons.

As I stated, Gareth's book is next. There's not much I can share because it's not written yet; all I have are a bunch of notes to myself. What I can say is, Gareth's story is my winter book of my *Love's Own Timeline* Series and the story will be told from Gareth's POV and I'm looking forward to spending time in his mind as I conjure this book. The only other item I can offer is the main trope is enemies-to-lovers which Gareth needs to work around.

Finally, thank you for finding and reading *Mine*, and taking a chance on this indie author. I hope you love Genevieve and Asher as much as I do. I appreciate you beyond words. Truly.

X🤍X🤍

Stephanie

The Soundtrack of Mine

Leather and Lace by Stevie Nicks (1982)
All the Things She Said by Simple Minds (1985)
I Just Want to Be Your Everything by Andy Gibb (1977)
Back to Friends by Sombr (2024)
Mayonnaise by Smashing Pumpkins (1993)
In Your Eyes by Peter Gabriel (1985)
Black by Pearl Jam (1991)
Creep by Radiohead (1992)
Fade Into You by Mazzy Star (1993)
The Ghost in You by The Psychedelic Furs (1984)
Dying by Hole (1998)
Pictures of You by The Cure (1989)
Fell on Black Days by Soundgarden (1994)
Iris by Goo Goo Dolls (1998)